SHROUD₅

You are holding a limited edition small press publication in your hands.
This book is a result of hard work and creative effort.
Enjoy it and celebrate the possibility of all things.

First Edition

First Printing March 2009

Copyright © 2009 Shroud Publishing

All Rights Reserved

The individual copyrights of the respective authors herein
reverted back to the original copyright holder upon publication.

Cover Art by Malcolm McClinton

ISBN: 978-1442123441

Designed and Printed in the USA

SP
Shroud
Publishing

www.shroudmagazine.com

Shroud Publishing LLC

121 Mason Rd.

Milton, NH 03851

SHROUD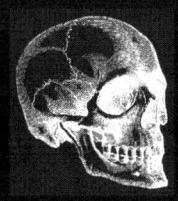

Shroud 5, Winter 2009

CONTENTS

Fiction

BUDDHA IN THE BOX Kim Paffenroth	7
FOR HER Michael West	22
THE PATH John Bruni	60
INSIDE THE BOX Nate Southard	86
GHOSTLY FOOTSTEPS Norman A. Rubin	98

Nonfiction

FROM THE EDITOR	4
DARK EFFIGIES: Malcolm McClinton Tim Deal	12
FRITZ LIEBER: SMOKE, GHOSTS & TERROR Daniel R. Robichaud	30
AUTHOR SPOTLIGHT: Ronald Damien Malfi Tim Lieder	40
WALK LIKE THE DEAD Conor Powers-Smith	50
MARKET REPORT: Necrotic Tissue D.L. Snell	68
HAUNTINGS, FREAKS & MYSTERIES Steve Vernon	75
PROGKNOSTICATIONS: Nate Southard Michael Knost	84
SPECIALTY PRESS SHOWCASE: Cargo Cult Press Norm Rubenstein	92

The Journal of Dark Fiction and Art

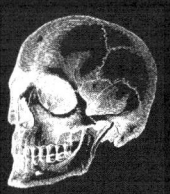

Publisher
Shroud Publishing LLC

Editor
Timothy P. Deal

Assistant Editors
Robert Canipe
Christa M. Miller

Marketing
Jennifer N. Deal

Layout and Design
Danny Evarts

Contributing Editors
Michael Knost
I.E. Lester
Kevin Lucia
Norman Rubenstein
DL Snell
Steve Vernon

Contributing Artists
Danny Evarts
Malcolm McClinton

Cover Art
Malcolm McClinton

ISSN
1940-7025

Copyright © 2009 by Shroud Publishing LLC. Individual works are copyright © 2009 by their respective creators. All rights reserved.

The Hiram Grange Chronicles

HIRAM GRANGE & THE VILLAGE OF THE DAMNED Jake Burrows	8
GEOGRAPHICAL CONFLUENCE Marie O'Regan & Paul Kane	16
HIRAM GRANGE & THE TWELVE LITTLE HITLERS Scott Christian Carr	35
HIRAM GRANGE & THE DIGITAL EUCHARIST Robert Davies	44
WEBLEY MARK VI REVOLVER Marie O'Regan	67
HIRAM GRANGE & THE CHOSEN ONE Kevin Lucia	70
WORMWOOD: THE WORLD OF THE GREEEN FAIRY Marie O'Regan	88
HIRAM GRANGE & THE BEAST OF THE AIR Richard Wright	102

Reviews

COVENANT John Everson	77
CRIMSON Gord Rollo	77
DARK HOLLOW and GHOST WALK Brian Keene	78
FROZEN BLOOD Joel A. Sutherland	79
JAKE'S WAKE John Skipp & Cody Goodfellow	80
JOHNNY GRUESOME Gregory Lamberson	80
SHEEP & WOLVES Jeremy C. Shipp	81
SUCCULENT PREY Wrath James White	82
JUST LIKE HELL Nate Southard	87

Games

LEFT 4 DEAD for PC & XBox 360 (Valve)	58

From The Editor:
The Scandalous Misadventures of Hiram Grange

There are dozens of e-mails in my in-box that proclaim, "I love Hiram," a subject line that served as a quick identifier for the exchange of ideas, snippets of text, and rough drafts among the group of authors that I tenderly refer to as the *Hiram Five*. As we built Hiram Grange we tried to avoid Dr. Frankenstein's mistake of cobbling life together through the use of spare parts. We wanted Hiram to be unique, more the product of a petri dish than a construct of other peoples' parts. As his odd lanky frame grew and developed, and his nuanced predilection to Jodie Foster started to manifest, we did indeed begin to "love" him. He became both everything that we are as well as everything that we are not. He shouldered our vilest obsessions yet demonstrated those traits—honor, bravery and sacrifice—that we would hope to possess. Most of all, he has become the focus of our vicarious pursuits—a vehicle by which our (literally) wildest dreams may come true and our darkest fears may lurk.

I think it's only fair that I tell you up front that Hiram is far from perfect. He's a drug addict. He's an alcoholic. He's a licentious, irritable louse who would rather drink, smoke and rut than do ANYTHING else. Furthermore, he's not much to look at. However, for all of his flaws, Hiram stands watch over the forces of evil that threaten to slip from the Abyss into our world. He endeavors to interdict the malevolent assault of creatures of shadow, and well… sometimes succeeds.

I'll admit that pitting a surly antihero against the forces of the supernatural is not an entirely original literary trope. However, in creating Hiram and his world, the *Hiram Five* sought to develop complex and flawed characters, and then place them in a well researched and believable setting—even if that setting was, at times, fictional or speculative. In the end, *The Scandalous Misadventures of Hiram Grange* propels readers through a series of briskly paced and thrilling supernatural adventures featuring characters that will evoke a chuckle, grin or snarl. Also, we hit the jackpot by signing on the exceptionally talented Malcolm McClinton as the artist behind the adventure. Malcolm's art graces the cover to this issue.

Use this issue of *Shroud* to familiarize yourself with Hiram's world. Learn about geographic confluences, strip down the Webley Mark VI, or sample the Green Fairy. Then dive into one of the five novella excerpts to see Hiram in action and discover for yourself whether or not you too could possibly, just remotely, against all better judgment… love Hiram.

But that's not all. We are thrilled and honored to have exciting new fiction from Kim Paffenroth, Michael West, John Bruni, and Norman A. Rubin, as well as an interview with Ronald Damien Malfi, and columns from Michael Knost, Steve Vernon and Norman Rubenstein. We also have a whole slew of reviews from I.E. Lester and new contributing editor Kevin Lucia, and an eye-catching new layout by our friend and designer Danny Evarts. Yes, folks, the woodcuts and prints you see throughout are real and they are Danny's.

I sincerely hope you enjoy this issue of *Shroud*, and as always, thank you for your continued support!

—Tim Deal
Editor/Publisher

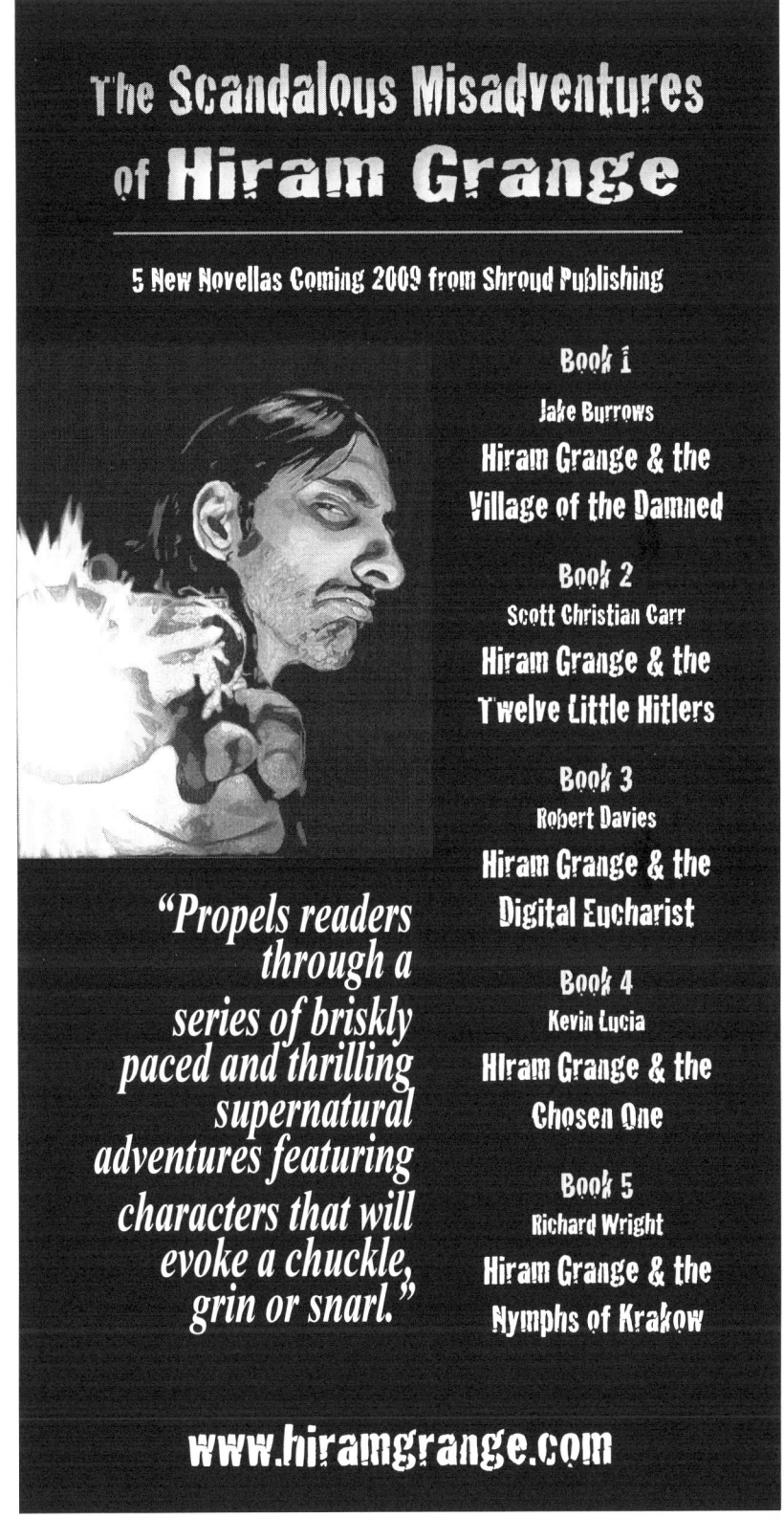

KIM PAFFENROTH
BUDDHA IN THE BOX

Stan bent down and pulled the trunk release latch next to the driver's seat. He had to open it, after seeing the car rocking, with banging and moaning coming from inside the trunk. As the trunk popped, the old Chinese guy rounded the corner of the gas station, returning from the men's room. The old man raised his arms and yelled as Stan leaped toward the back of the car to help whoever was in there.

The thing in the trunk lunged. A long, white ponytail whipped over Stan's right shoulder as the thing's teeth tore into his neck. He screamed and struggled with the figure, which seemed to be a man so emaciated he was like a corpse, his head shaved except for the long ponytail, his clothes stiff rags, his nails dirty claws, and an oppressive stench coming off him. Then, suddenly, the assailant shuddered and released its hold on Stan.

Clutching his neck, Stan staggered back and fell to the pavement, the blood pouring between his fingers hot and silky, though the wound itself felt icy. The Chinese man stood above him, holding a shovel that Stan had left leaning against the gas station's wall. He gave the corpse-thing another smack in the head with it; it growled slightly. After that it sat calmly in the trunk, looking almost like the pictures of Buddha that Stan had seen when he took a World Civilizations course at the community college—a placid, stiff figure with frozen features and blank eyes. A notable difference was the bloody smear around its mouth.

The man with the shovel leaned it against one of the pumps and picked up the gas nozzle. "My great-grandfather was a very bad man," he began. "Drugs, prostitution, gambling—he preyed on everyone in our community, so much that they cursed him with this existence that is neither life nor death. Only if his descendants took him away and atoned for his crimes for three generations would the curse be lifted. I am taking him back to San Francisco for that ceremony."

The figure in the trunk coiled itself back up and the other man closed the trunk. The cold now reached from Stan's eyes to his stomach. "I know—why bother for such a wretched creature? His lack of piety and honor does not absolve us from their dictates." Stan's eyes widened as gasoline poured from the nozzle. "I am sorry I cannot save you as well. Did you open the car out of curiosity and compassion?" No sound came when Stan moved his mouth. "Those are part of Buddha-nature, and I sense them in you, young man. For that, at least, we can be glad." The man dropped the nozzle and got back into his car.

Stan heard the engine, then the tires crunching on the gravel. As the cold overwhelmed the last of his impure body, the flames found the perfect fuel of his spirit.

Kim Paffenroth is a professor of religious studies and the author of several books on the Bible and theology. He first garnered attention in the horror field with his 2006 Bram Stoker Award winning *Gospel of the Living Dead: George Romero's Visions of Hell on Earth* (Baylor, 2006). He has since gone on to publish *Dying to Live: A Novel of Life among the Undead* (Permuted Press, 2007), *Orpheus and the Pearl* (Magus Press, 2008), and *Dying to Live: Life Sentence* (Permuted Press, 2008).

More on Kim can be found at *gotld.blogspot.com*.

Excerpt from...

Hiram Grange & the Village of the Damned

Jake Burrows

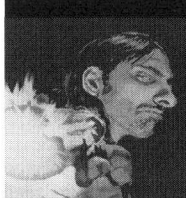

Hiram was a man with a pragmatic disposition and specific tastes.

There were three things that Hiram Grange was compelled to do before opening the door of his vintage Airstream trailer and venturing out into the world. He had to sip a glass of absinthe to the crackling strains of Wagner played on his old Victrola; he had to smoke a quarter gram of opium in his favorite briarwood pipe (between sips); and he had to vigorously masturbate to a well-worn 8x10 glossy of Jodie Foster.

The absinthe he bought in Fayence, France, the opium he acquired from a dealer with Taliban ties in Boston, and the photograph was acquired on eBay some years prior. The sources rarely, if ever, varied, nor did his pre-departure ritual. These three things quieted his nerves enough for him to face the world and all of its evils.

In Hiram's world, the evils often outweighed the good, the decent or even the normal.

Once fully prepared, Hiram would wash his long bony hands, comb his oily black hair, slip his twelve inch knife in the sheath in the small of his back, and fasten his Webley breaktop in the holster under his left arm. He would regard himself in the full-length mirror behind the door, seemingly unaware that his black suit with the three-quarter length jacket and the wilting bow-tie was both ill-fitting and disastrously out of fashion.

His reflection betrayed a man of indeterminable age who was comprised of an all-too-pale assemblage of awkward bone-thin limbs that congregated at angular joints. Besides his tall, lanky stature, his other most obvious feature jutted out between and slightly below two intensely blue eyes—his nose. Its length was frightening and cartoon like—a caricature of a nose; someone's idea of a practical joke, a mass of hair-sprouting cartilage the likes of which have not been seen before on man nor beast.

Not that it mattered much anyway, for Hiram realized long ago that he would always be (disastrously or not) *Hiram*—a fate that many would consider literally far worse than death.

Hiram was not a man that one took at face value. For behind, and a little above, that huge proboscis was a shrewd intellect and an encyclopedic knowledge of the darker parts of the world. He was man that was both consumed with fear but was absolutely resolute when it came to dispensing violence. He pursued his twisted and perverse desires, but selflessly risked his life to maintain the Earth's spiritual equilibrium; furthermore, he was a man that one could trust with his life, but (as they say) not with one's money and certainly never (*ever*) with one's wife.

He steeled his nerves and grabbed the well-stocked leather knapsack hanging by the door. If he had any choice in the matter he would simply lay about the house all day in an absinthe and opium-induced haze and use the time to concoct a plan for finally meeting Jodie Foster in person. But alas, his life was not his own to waste, and choice was an impulse that had long since been taken from him. He was merely an indentured servant—the property of others, and as such, freewill was a carrot waived tauntingly in front of his massive nose.

Before he left, he almost forgot. He hastened over to his cheap plastic Korean stereo and pulled a cassette from the deck. He popped it into a plastic case, the label of which was thick with his scrawl. Sighing deeply, he unfastened, unbolted and unchained the locks that protected him from the outside world, and pitched himself purposefully into the day.

Deep within his trouser pocket lay a crumpled missive outlining detailed instructions for Hiram to follow. They involved a convoluted and tiresome series of conveyances intended to throw possible interlopers off of his tracks. There followed an equally exhausting series of encoded dead drop locations, prepaid cell phone calls, pay phone calls, Internet café chat room meetings, and back-room bar rendezvous in shady districts and hazardous boroughs. Such notes were a nuisance to Hiram. He had been performing his duties for decades, and his line of work seldom required these measures—a testament to the unique nature of his vocation, if not the criticality of it.

He would follow the instructions, but along the way he never failed to discretely inform his handler, the fastidious and punctual Mrs. Bothwell, that he was on *Hiram's* schedule, and Hiram's schedule allowed for unplanned deviations in course, and those deviations invariably would include some type of Thai massage parlor, an opium den, or failing these—a live sex show. Hiram needed these diversions to reaffirm his humanness—his connection with the race he so ardently fought to protect, or, at least, this is what he told Bothwell.

But before he did anything, he would stop into *UberNacht*, his favorite dive, and catch up with Sadie. Sadie was 22 and a self-professed daughter of the night. Her passion for things dark ranged from horror movies to her rare collection of Lovecraft and Derleth correspondence. She was slight and pale with mournful brown eyes trimmed in black eyeliner beneath a Betty Page hairstyle. Her wit was finely honed and her intellect supported by a prolific reading habit. Hiram's relationship with her was simple—she was the only human being he could tolerate, and he was the only human being that did not bore the absolute shit out of her.

UberNacht was a short cab ride from his "home" and located downtown in the old industrial district where derelict factories and old warehouses became the trendy digs to scores of artists, writers and Beat revivalists. The bar sat below street level beneath a city-sponsored syringe exchange. It was early for *UberNacht* and as Hiram walked into the dark, cave-like environment there was but a smattering of clientele. He found his usual corner unoccupied and he sat. Sadie was upon him immediately, replete in a black tank, plaid schoolgirl's skirt, red and white striped thigh-highs, and 8-eyelet Doc Martins with red laces.

"Mr. Wells, it's early for you. You catch that maudlin performance by Hillary last night? She got all teary during one of her campaign speeches. A real Oprah moment for her. Made me want to puke. I had to switch over to a *Twilight Zone* rerun—you want the green stuff or the brown stuff today?"

Hiram smiled inwardly at the "Mr. Wells" reference—a pet name she had applied to him because his initials were "HG." He pulled the cassette out of his breast pocket and handed it to her.

"This one has some *Fields of the Nephilim*, *A Split Second*, and that *Sisters of Mercy* Bootleg from Berlin I told you about. Side two is mostly *Bauhaus*, but I threw in some *Mission UK* to finish up the space. If you liked *The Mission*, you'll love *The Mission UK*."

Sadie grabbed the tape and thrust it dramatically into her slight cleavage.

"I will listen to it during a hot bath and a cold razor my friend. So, what'll it be?"

"The brown," Hiram replied.

Sadie zipped away and returned with a single malt scotch and a folded piece of poster board. She laid the glass down and handed the poster board to Hiram. He took it enthusiastically. He opened it to find a detailed collage of Jodie Foster taken from a variety of color and black-and-white magazine clippings. Hiram's thick lips widened into a grin. Sadie's collages were always magnificent—each one better than the last—and this one featured some of Jodie's most recent appearances.

"You spoil me." He said.

"I had some time on my hands."

Hiram's chest tightened a little and his pale skin reddened. It did not matter that Sadie routinely presented him with these elaborate collages, each offering made him feel awkward and strange. He was, and always would be, unaccustomed to her generosity. It was not just the gift, but her acknowledgement and tacit approval of an obsession that was best left secret. It was months earlier that several single malts had resulted in the revelation of his desire to be with Jodie Foster, and instead of characterizing him as a sick "stalker" she merely nodded and accepted it. "Whatever gets you out of bed in the morning," she had said. It was that live and let live attitude that endeared Sadie to him and allowed him to open up—to an extent. He could never tell her about his job, not everything at least, not the gory and strange details; she would think him completely off his rocker.

Bloody hell, he thought, he *was* off his rocker

Sadie nodded towards his knapsack. "Business trip?"

"I'm auditing a grant-funded research project out of Rutgers. Bloody tiresome task, but someone has to keep these mad scientists fiscally responsible."

"Sounds absolutely miserable my friend," she said. "Try not to over medicate yourself out of boredom."

Hiram finished his scotch and pulled out a heavy watch fob. He could not delay the inevitable any longer. He pulled a twenty from his wallet and left it on the table.

"I'll look in on you when I return," he said, rising out of his booth to leave.

Sadie smiled. "*Nell* is on Sunday night—I'll TiVo it for you."

To be continued in
Hiram Grange & the Village of the Damned....

Jake Burrows is the author of more than 100 articles, stories, and essays published in a variety of mediums and publications spanning the globe, under various pen names. He is a former Police Constable from West Clare, Ireland and a former Intelligence Specialist with the Irish Defence Forces Directorate of Intelligence, also known as G2. In his spare time he enjoys traveling. Jake spends about half of his time in the United States where he owns a small cottage overlooking Great Bay New Hampshire. He is also quite fond of reading, hiking, music, art, history and single malt whiskeys.

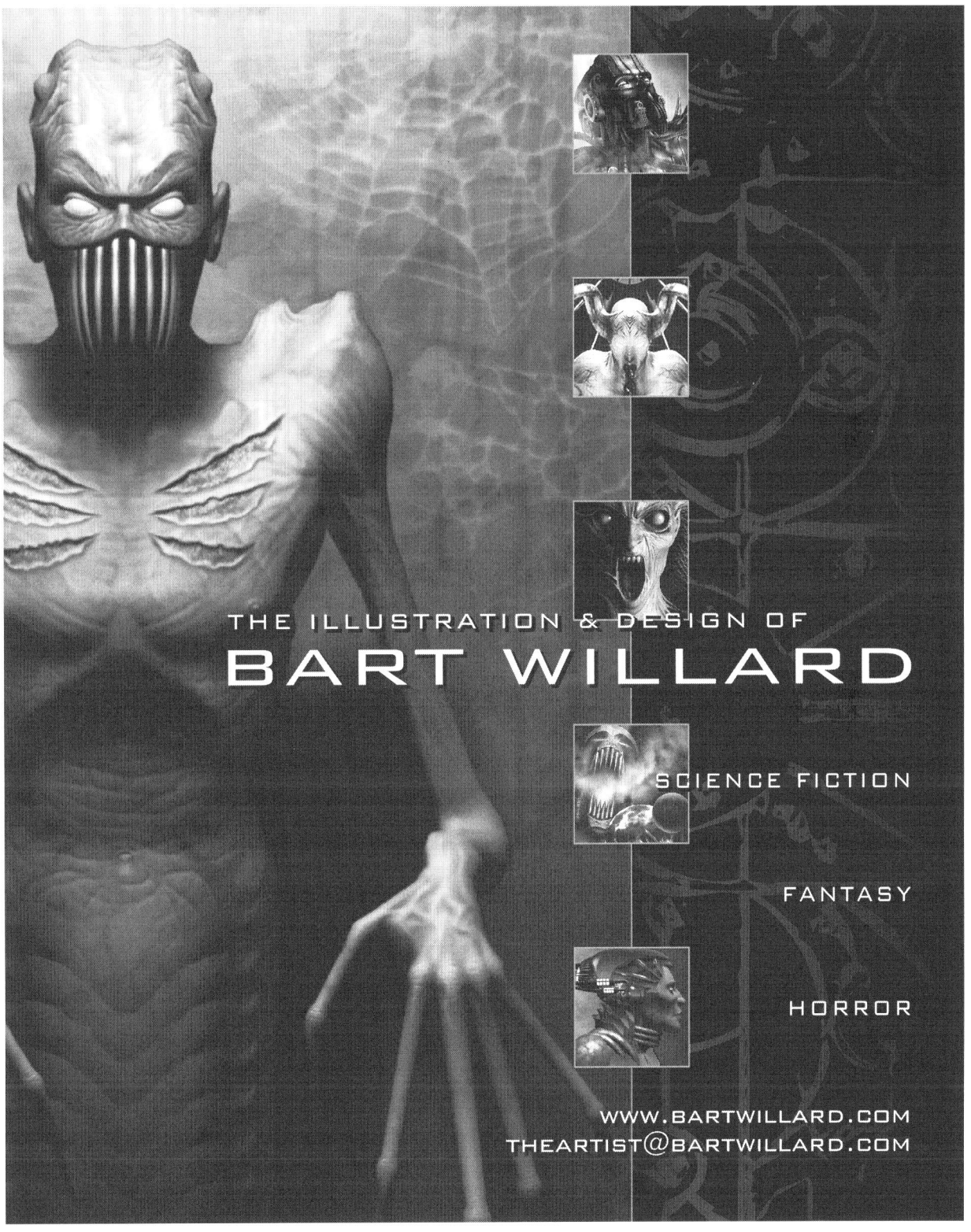

An Interview with Malcolm McClinton
by Tim Deal

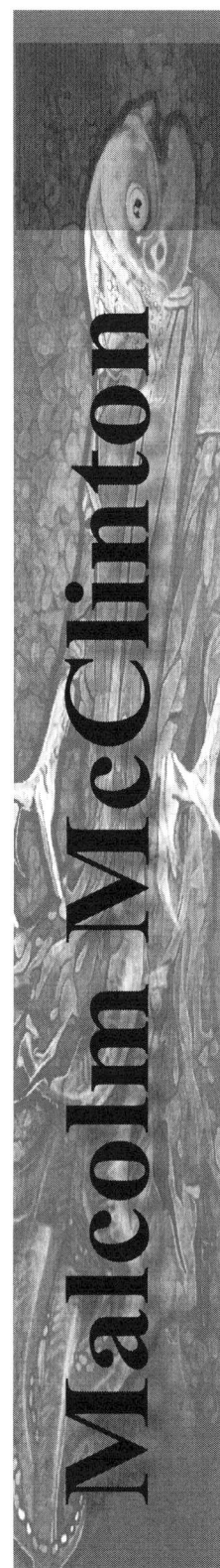

Malcolm McClinton has been drawing and painting science fiction and fantasy subjects as long as he can remember, but until 9 or so years ago illustrating it was only a hobby, something he would do to relax. Most of his efforts had been in academics. After earning advance degrees in Physical Anthropology and Archaeology he spent five or six years working out in the field excavating. However, he experienced burn out and took a job at Dark Horse Comics managing their prepress department. Looking at all the really cool and beautiful art that passed through his department re-ignited his creative drive and after three years he left to pursue his own painting and projects. He has been illustrating as a means of making a living ever since. He has since found a nice little niche for himself that satisfies his "anti-authority nature, reclusiveness and need for adulation" all at once.

SHROUD: Who are some of your influences?

MALCOLM: Comic books (70s and 80s artists, like Berry Windsor Smith and Bernie Wrightson, Jeffrey Jones and Neil Adams), Art Nouveau, and Pre Raphaelites are all very strong influences on my art, both in terms of style and what I like to paint. I think that is what makes my art a little un-hip. Every now and then I try to create something a little more cutting edge, but it usually fails. I comfort myself by the notion that, as styles and tastes continually cycle, someday me and my art will be hip—providing I live that long.

SHROUD: What kind of art were you creating in your 7th grade art class?

MALCOLM: Kind of embarrassing, but I was pretty much drawing the same kind of stuff—myths, monsters and women.

SHROUD: What was/is your preferred media?

MALCOLM: I will always love watercolor and I will still sometimes do portions of an image using those traditional mediums, scan them in to the computer and integrate them into digitally generated images. But, I feel that working on the computer has really freed my art.

SHROUD: Favorite 1980s teen comedy?

MALCOLM: Truth is, in the 80's I was in college and grad school and a little past teen TV. I was more of a *Hill Street Blues*, *Cheers* sort of guy.

SHROUD: Favorite 1970s horror flick?

Dark Effigies
Artists within the Genre

MALCOLM: Alien—Not only is it one of the greatest horror films, it is also one of the best sci-fi movies ever made. Through out the 70's horror had gone from the old studio monster and radioactive mutant giant—you pick the insect—to the don't look now he's behind you female mutilation, sexually charged slasher movies. Alien turned that trend on its head. Ripley is the strong female character who makes active judgments and survives what is trying to kill her. The male characters are largely passive—most die quickly, others wait for her command. It is Ripley who makes the plan to defeat the alien which works, while the "powerless" male Captain makes bad judgments as his unsure plan fails. Her sexuality is derived from her strength rather then from her vulnerability—I love that.

SHROUD: Name three things that absolutely terrify you.

MALCOLM: Getting a 9-to-5 Job

Cocktail parties

Interviews (shudder)

SHROUD: Can you give us the evolution of your current technique?

MALCOLM: How I create my images could be used as a guide in art school on how not to illustrate.

For instance, I hate to do preliminary sketches. I tend to work in a more free-form organic way. I have a general idea of the image but no firm picture of what I want it to look like. Usually I start by creating a central character and build out from there. I often do very large and complex scenes, involving multiple characters and battles, and I am often surprised by the direction and shape that my images take as they grow and expand across my canvas.

I started out working primarily with watercolor and color pencil, but I have gradually migrated to using the computer. Because of its transparent nature, watercolor is such an unforgiving medium and you can imagine this method of creating images leads to lots of problems and starting over.

But once I started using the computer and had the ability to undo and try again, I have become much more experimental. The whole process is now more dynamic and spontaneous. I will create each element in the image, their shading and highlights are on different layers (some of my more complex images have upward of 300 layers). That way I can move elements around the canvas, change their lighting, put

Hiram Grange Cover Art for *Shroud* 5 by Malcolm McClinton

them in the background, or move them to the front. It is a lot like stage-blocking a scene for a play, and in a real sense my newer stuff has a more cinematic feel to it.

I have found working on the computer has made me a much bigger risk taker then ever before. These last years have been some of the most exciting for me as a creator in a very long time.

SHROUD: Where do you find your subjects—people objects locations?

MALCOLM: Where I get inspiration for subjects? Well obviously when I do commissioned work the ideas come from the story, or the publishers, or the authors. There is often a discussion as to what would be the best scene to illustrate, and sketches and approvals and all that. When I am just drawing for fun the ideas can come from Movies, books, myths, stories that I have made up, other artists—really ideas come from just about anywhere. For instance, I am working on an image now that was inspired by a young woman walking down the street. She was dressed in a black t-shirt and black knee high leggings and pink converse tennis shoes. She sported a baseball bat over her shoulder and a walk that warned against any one messing with her. She had a kind of retro/vigilante/superhero feel about her. Her shortish hair covered much of face, so I could not really see her features that well, but I made contact with her one visible eye and it told me she knew that she was hot and that I was definably not in her league. "Wow," I thought, "I want to be with her when the Zombies attack." That inspired an illustration featuring a woman in black, with pink converse shoes, surrounded by zombies, wielding a couple baseball bats—I think at heart I am a storyteller. Its just that my medium is pictures instead of words.

SHROUD: Tell us two things no one knows about you.

MALCOLM: I like sissy drinks—White Russians, Appletinis—the sweeter the better

I don't think I know you well enough to tell you the other, maybe after a few more drinks, oh wait is this a cocktail party? Aaaaaaah!!!

SHROUD: Where can we expect to see your work in 2009? What direction are you planning to take your art?

MALCOLM: For the first few years of illustrating professionally I was kind of trapped in a role-playing and collectible card game ghetto, over the last couple of last years I have been able to break out, doing concept work and posters for small independent films and video games. Book covers became a primary source of work, I got the chance to do comic book pin-ups and covers, and illustrations for a high end clothing company. I am really hoping to build on this in the coming year.

What would be a dream, though, would be able to work on my own projects and bring them to fruition, but right now I pretty much have to work non stop on paying projects to make a living at this illustration thing.

SHROUD: How did Hiram manifest visually for you?

MALCOLM: Tim sent me a few chapters from the first book and Hiram sort of exploded from my head full blown. I think he had been hanging out in the darker regions of my brain all along, drinking absinthe and waiting. It would certainly explain some of the more disturbing dreams I have had.

In truth, I credit the Hiram Five for coming up with such a vivid character. While some projects are just jobs to pay the mortgage and buy food, there are other projects that I am really excited about and feel privileged to be a part of. I think Hiram Grange is that kind of project—the stories are visual, raw, gritty, violent, funny and more then a little seedy, with supernatural monsters, hot chicks and are very, very cool.

GEOGRAPHICAL CONFLUENCE

BY MARIE O'REGAN & PAUL KANE

What is now known by the blanket term "paranormal activity" has been with us throughout the ages. Hauntings, possessions, psychic phenomena such as precognition or telepathy or even EVP (Electronic Voice Phenomena); there are many variations. But there has also long been discussion about whether such activity is, for want of a better word, "enhanced" in places where a specific occurrence has impacted on its surroundings–a natural disaster, an accident or a murder. Although there is no concrete proof at this time that would satisfy even the most ardent of disbelievers, here we look at just some of these occurrences, and the claims surrounding them.

JACK THE RIPPER

The location of Jack the Ripper's famous murders, Whitechapel, has itself become something of a destination for those interested in the macabre over the years. And who could blame people? It was here that Jack brutally murdered a number of women in the late nineteenth century, severing throats, cutting open abdomens and even relieving victims of their organs.

Little wonder then, that the area has gained the reputation of being haunted. One of the hot spots in this regard is definitely *The Ten Bells pub*. It was here that Jack's final victim, Mary Kelly, spent her last evening alive – leaving in the early hours of November 9, 1888. Her horrifically mutilated body was found the next morning in Millers Court of Dorset Street, just opposite *The Ten Bells*.

Capitalising on the legend, the pub was renamed *The Jack the Ripper* in the 1970s and 80s – and even served a drink called "The Ripper's Tipple" – though it reverted back to its original name in 1989. During the 90s and into the 2000s, increased supernatural activity was reported at the pub. Live-in staff said they saw a man in Victorian clothing, and would often wake up in the middle of the night with a sense that someone was in the room (occasionally some even reported seeing a ghost on the bed beside them). One tenant in particular reported hearing footsteps and loud laughter outside his door, although when he opened it he would always find the corridor empty. Often, when down in the bar, he would also feel himself being pushed back as if by an invisible hand.

The pub was investigated first by a psychic, who said that she could feel that something "terrible had happened" in one of the rooms involving the death of an infant. Then Lindsay Siviter, top researcher and authority on Jack the Ripper, was looking around in the roof of the pub when she found some material trapped in the floor behind the water tank. Tugging at it, she discovered it was a sack tied securely at the top – and inside were the mouldy remains of Victorian baby clothes, apparently slashed with a knife. The water tank was slap bang over the room that the psychic had earlier referred to.

SPECTRES OF WAR

Most people are familiar with the story that Arthur Machen wrote during the First World War, "The Bowmen"–indeed, it has been the inspiration for further tales, such as the recent excellent novella from Tim Lebbon and Simon Clark, *Exorcising Angels*. While working as a journalist, Machen published an "account" in The Evening News in 1914, positing that the ghosts of otherworldly bowmen were at work during The Battle of Mons, where the British Army were being driven back by overwhelming German forces. Though fiction, it was taken as fact by many readers and linked into apparently genuine rumours from the front that it was angels who had come to the aid of the Brits. It spawned a whole mythology which eventually boiled the whole thing down to the Angel of Mons—a single towering spirit that appeared to drive away the Hun.

Over the years it has been mentioned in many histories of the First World War; for example in Daniel David's book *The 1914 Campaign* he says that, "Some beleaguered soldiers reported being rescued by angels and ghostly bowmen." Though no official reports mention the phenomenon, there is evidence in existence that German prisoners also described a force of phantoms armed with bows and arrows. It's unlikely whether anyone will be able to prove without a shadow of a doubt whether or not "something" did happen during that bloody battle, but it's nevertheless interesting to speculate that the many deaths gave rise to a supernatural event of some kind. After all, there's a long history of such paranormal activity linked to war.

Ancient Greek scribes once wrote about the plains of Marathon, where Athenian Infantrymen fought the Persians in 490 BC. But for years afterwards visitors to the fields said they could hear the screams of the dying or the whistle of spears. After The Battle of Edgehill in 1642 – part of the English Civil War – there were reports that the dead soldiers from the battlefield rose up out of the earth right in front of survivors.

> "INHABITANTS CLAIMED THAT FOR A LONG TIME AFTER THE WAR HAD FINISHED THEY BORE WITNESS TO JAPANESE GHOSTS IN RUSTY HELMETS RISING UP TO MAN AN OLD ANTI-AIRCRAFT GUN THAT WAS LEFT ABANDONED ON THE BEACH..."

In the 18th century, too, people allegedly saw heavenly creatures at Culloden and then on two occasions at the battle of Souter Fell. And in the South Pacific, which saw its fair share of battles during World War II, many cases of supernatural activity have been logged in the subsequent decades.

In the late 1950s, for example, a reporter for the BBC said that he'd experienced a haunting in a house in Kuala Selangor, Malaysia – which had once been occupied by Japanese officers. He claimed that the property still reverberated with the sounds of heavy military-issue boots. Then there were the reports that fishermen on the island of Corregidor in the Philippines had seen spectral patrols for years after the war. That same island's port of Hollandia had actually been the site of a major Allied invasion in the spring of 1944, and inhabitants claimed that for a long time after the war had finished they bore witness to Japanese ghosts in rusty helmets rising up to man an old anti-aircraft gun that was left abandoned on the beach. This last tale was even picked up by Reuters News Agency! Mass hallucinations? Or something more?

There just might be a correlation between the casualties of war and unexplained activity like this. Especially when you consider the number of people who've visited the sites of former warzones and said they "felt" something.

LIZZIE BORDEN LIVES

Lizzie Borden took an ax
Gave her mother forty whacks;
When she saw what she had done
Gave her father forty-one!

A rhyme that refers to the legend of Lizzie Borden, famous for allegedly taking a hatchet to her father and stepmother, Andrew and Abbey, killing them both.

Although she was never convicted, public opinion was firm—She was guilty. She lived the rest of her life quietly, until she died in Fall River, Massachusetts, of pneumonia in 1927.

The house where the murders took place, however, is reputed

Illustration by Tom Moran for Michael McBride's *Remains*. Published by Cargo Cult Press. See article on pg. 92.

to be haunted to this day. Although the house remained a private residence for some time after the murders, today it is a Bed and Breakfast hotel, the Lizzie Borden Bed and Breakfast, and as with the sites of most famous murders, you can even do a "ghost tour" of the property.

Many guests staying here have reported hearing a woman sobbing at nighttime. Some have even seen shoes move across a room – *Poltergeist* style – while others have claimed that a ghost has "tucked them in" at night, by all accounts Lizzie's murdered stepmother. In addition, lights flicker, TV and videos switch themselves on and off, and cameras take photographs on their own—further evidence that the ghosts of Andrew and Abbey Borden still inhabit that place, and that because of the way they were killed the house is prone to more supernatural occurrences than others.

GRAVE CONCERNS

Speaking of *Poltergeist*, the movie may have been fantasy but as we all know a lot of fiction is based in truth. Indian burial grounds have long been a cliché in horror, but there can be no disputing their links to paranormal activity.

One such location is Robinson Woods, named after Alexander Robinson (the English name of Chee-Chee-Pin-Quay, Chief of the Potawatomi, Chippewa and Ottawa Indian tribes). In his colourful life, Robinson helped to save John Kinzie, Captain and Mrs. Heald and their families from the bloodbath that came about due to the destruction of Fort Dearborn in 1812. In 1829, in the treaty of Prairie du Chien, Robson was given "two sections on the Rivere Aux Pleins above and adjoining the tract herein granted to Claude La Gramboise" where he lived with his French wife and children.

His descendants resided there until the mid-1950s, when their property burned to the ground in mysterious circumstances and Robinson's granddaughter, aged 89, had to be rescued by firemen. The place has never been the same since. Later that year, three young boys were murdered after leaving a northwest side bowling alley, their naked bodies found in Robinson Woods.

Investigations into the area (now called The Robinson Family Burial Grounds), sparked by consistent reports of strange events, have yielded extremely interesting results. On one occasion recording devices were left at the site, and when played back the tapes clearly picked up an Indian tom-tom being played! Add to this bizarre lights seen from the road, the sound of chopping wood (the last of the Robinsons were always out doing this activity) and a distinctive smell near the burial ground—that of lilacs or violets; even in winter, when there are no flowers in bloom. It's a smell that apparently hovers well above the ground and is not affected in the slightest by the breeze and absolutely cannot be explained.

NATURAL DISASTER

Turning now to "Acts of God," as people call them. Like the previous entries, these often result in deaths and therefore increased paranormal activity. One of the most recent and most relevant examples is the devastation caused by Hurricane Katrina. Already noted for its supernatural activity and links to voodoo, New Orleans is known for its excellent ghost tours - and The Lalaurie House (where the mistress Madame Lalaurie once treated slaves brutally back in the early part of the 19th century) is generally considered to be one of the most haunted locations in the world.

But the events of 2005, when Hurricane Katrina—one of the deadliest and most costly hurricanes of all time (the sixth strongest overall in recorded Atlantic hurricane history)—would

> "ON ONE OCCASION RECORDING DEVICES WERE LEFT AT THE SITE, AND WHEN PLAYED BACK THE TAPES CLEARLY PICKED UP AN INDIAN TOM-TOM BEING PLAYED!"

definitely bolster that reputation. With at least 1,836 dead from Katrina itself, or the subsequent flooding, New Orleans was devastated and left a ghost town… in more ways than one.

In the aftermath of the disaster, members of the U.S. military were sent in to help and reported getting the feeling that they were "not alone." At one spot in particular, the Sophie B. Wright Middle School, a chaplain was moved to utter, "In the name of Jesus Christ, I command you Satan to leave the dark areas of this building." Sgt. Robin Hairston of the California National Guard had this to say on a CBS5 broadcast in San Francisco. "I was in my sleeping bag and I opened my eyes and in the doorway was a little girl… It wasn't my imagination."

SPC. Rosales Leanor, meanwhile, had her own story to tell. "I was using the restroom and I just saw a little shadow, kind of looming in front of me." Another Guard unit member claimed she spotted a little girl and heard her laughing when she opened a closet containing cleaning supplies. Other reports included a number of Bibles being found in different locations, all open at the book of Revelations.

POSSESSIONS

There have been many reported cases of possession through the years—with no definitive proof as to whether any of them were actually real, although many people firmly believe that they are.

One of the most famous was the case that the movie *The Exorcist* was based on—the supposedly true story of fourteen-year-old Douglas Deen in Washington State in 1949. Although opinion is divided as to whether this was, in fact, a case of demon possession, a poltergeist or some other more natural event, the story persists and became the inspiration for Friedkin's 1973 movie; arguably the most disturbing movie of its kind, before or since, but possession remains one of the most emotive subjects in the paranormal canon. There are no further reports of hauntings at that house, though, so the possession in this case would seem to be of the boy rather than the place.

In contrast, and the subject of another film, the Amityville House is very definitely a case of a house believed to be the subject of demonic possession. There are rumours that the events portrayed in the novel *The Amityville Horror* (the basis for several movies), purported to be based on a true story, were faked for publicity; but certain elements of the story are a matter of fact, and verifiable.

The first fact is that in November 1974 the young Ronald De Feo shot his family, killing all six of them: his parents, two brothers and two sisters. The second fact is that De Feo claimed he did it because God told him to. He heard voices talking to him, and as no one was around, he reasoned that it must have been God.

So far, the story sounds like one of schizophrenia rather than of possession. A year after these events, though, the Lutz family moved in—only to flee the house twenty-eight days later claiming the house was possessed. According to the Lutzes, a whole catalogue of paranormal events occurred during that time: doors and windows banging with no reason; flies buzzing in a room in the dead of winter; slime oozing from doors and windows; toilet bowls turned black; phone contact was intermittent at best, with the family priest complaining his hands bled every time he tried to call them; the youngest daughter claimed to have befriended a huge, ghostly pig with red eyes that she called "Jodie"; not to mention the priest being told to "get out" by a ghostly voice when blessing the house shortly after the Lutzes moved in.

The Lutzes were introduced to author Jay Anson several months later, and the seeds of the novel were born. The book went on to spawn an entire franchise. There have been lawsuits and articles aplenty concerning the truthfulness of these claims, and we may never know for sure what the true facts are.

ELECTRONIC VOICE PHENOMENA(E.V.P)

Another form of paranormal event that has gained in prominence in recent years is that of E.V.P., or Electronic Voice Phenomena—a theory that the dead can still be heard, in the static or "white noise" that occurs on electrical appliances such as radios or televisions in between stations. Two movies based on this, *White Noise* and *White Noise 2: The Light*, were very successful in raising E.V.P's profile.

The process of trying to contact the dead in this manner actually began in the very early days of sound recording. Thomas Edison is known to have tried to make contact as far back as the 1890s, using a form of phonograph. There are claims that spirit voices were first captured on phonographic devices in 1938, after his death, but credit is commonly given to another man, Friedrich Jürgenson, who started his investigations in 1903. The story goes that he was recording birdsong one day, and on playing the tape back, was surprised to hear human voices—even though he had been the only person around at the time of recording. Intrigued, he experimented with recording what should have been empty air—but continued to record human voices. Eventually, in 1964, he published a book on the subject, Sprechfunk mit Verstorbenen (Translation: "Radio Link With The Dead").

Ghost hunters have visited famous U.S. prison, Alcatraz, on many occasions—and there are numerous examples online of instances of E.V.P. there. Even before the prison was built in 1859, Native Americans shunned "the rock," claiming it was home to evil spirits. The prison itself has a troubled history, and finally closed in 1963, but in its time such famous criminals as Al Capone, Frank "Machine Gun" Kelly and Robert Stroud (the Birdman of Alcatraz—something of a misnomer as he kept birds at Fort Leavenworth, not Alcatraz, and his nickname there was Bird Doctor of Leavenworth) were incarcerated there. Tapes have recorded screams, moans, names and even threats—although everything is open to interpretation.

Again, there is no definitive proof—and sceptics claim that what is being heard is really no more than a bleed-over from radio transmitters, or words heard because of the desire to hear them, nothing more. Whether E.V.P. is random noise or the dead trying to pass on messages to the living, the phenomenon would appear to be here to stay.

Marie O'Regan is a writer and freelance journalist, writing for magazines such as *Fortean Times*, *Writing Magazine*, *Writers' Forum*, *Dreamwatch*, *Death Ray*, *Dark Side*, *Rue Morgue*, *Red Scream* and *Hub*, among others. Marie is a regular contributor to *Shroud*. More on Marie can be found at www.marieoregan.net.

Paul Kane is author of the novel *Arrowhead*, along with several collections and novellas. His work has garnered several British Fantasy Society Award Recommendations, and he is editor of the *Shadow Writer* and *Terror Tales* anthologies. Current news on Paul's writings can be seen at www.shadow-writer.co.uk.

MICHAEL WEST
FOR HER

Brooke wanted to have a threesome.

Not that Jeff was complaining. Sex with two women at once was the fantasy of every straight, red-blooded American man. But as the Nevada highway unfurled beneath the glare of his headlights, and the time and place for the actual event drew nearer with each passing mile, a nervous dread nestled in the pit of his stomach, feeding him the same question again and again:

Does she want to leave me for someone else?

Brooke's appetite for sex was ravenous, insatiable, and despite five years of marriage, the ghosts of imagined infidelities still haunted the darkness at the back of Jeff's mind. He pictured her having affairs with men who were more muscular, or younger, or just plain *bigger* than he was, but in all of his insecure, paranoid delusions, he'd never once thought of her in bed with another woman.

Such a scenario suddenly played out behind his eyes, and he had to fight to maintain control of the Durango's wheel, his tires kicking up sand as they momentarily left the asphalt.

"Careful there, Tiger." Brooke's hand pressed the Mapquest directions flat against her muscular thigh. "I'd like to get there in one piece. Are you falling asleep?"

"Not on your life," he told her, managing a smile.

She grinned back and ran her fingers through her blonde mane, exposing the multitude of golden hoops that pierced her ear. The Japanese character for "love" was tattooed on the side of her neck, just above her left shoulder. Jeff glanced down at Brooke's hip, finding the latest addition to her body art collection peeking out from beneath the waistband of her shorts. A bright blue serpent with mottled, feathery wings etched onto its scaly back. She had it done the day she asked him to take her to this whorehouse.

At first, Jeff had been apprehensive. The idea of sex with a prostitute provoked nightmare visions where his cock turned black and rotted off. But Brooke wouldn't let it go, and she'd done her homework. The ladies, she'd told him, were tested prior to reporting for duty; they worked seven days straight, and could not leave the property for any reason during that shift; and since condom use was mandated by state law, there had been no cases—*zero*—where the customer of a legal brothel contracted a deadly disease. Finally, his wife showed him the profile of the working girl she had in mind—a curvy Latin lovely with the exotic name of Xilomen—and there was no way he could say no.

But Jeff couldn't stop wondering why she wanted it so badly.

He told himself it was just another kink she needed to get out of her system, and he was happy she hadn't gone behind his back to do it, happy she wanted him there to experience it with her.

Still, as Jeff chauffeured his wife toward this rendezvous with a woman they'd never met, he couldn't help but wonder if she secretly preferred women. He'd seen enough talk shows to know such things happened to people who'd been married much longer. Out of the blue, their spouses sat them down and told them they were gay. Either they had recently discovered feelings for someone of the same sex, or worse, they'd been fighting those longings their entire life, marrying only to conform to societal norms. It was a crazy idea, but he couldn't shake it, and it led him back to that same worrisome question:

Does she want to leave me for someone else?

Brooke read aloud from her directions, the stud that skewered her tongue glinting like a diamond as she spoke. "Turn left onto Cottontail Drive. Point one miles. End at the Bunny Hop Ranch."

He peered into the darkness at the edge of his headlights. "I don't suppose we'd be lucky enough to get a sign."

As if on cue, a flashing red speck illuminated the gloom ahead, growing larger and brighter as they approached until it became a blazing neon arrow, pointing them toward a dirt road. Beneath this arrow, a wooden billboard featured an airbrushed female rabbit in black lingerie. With its long eyelashes and glossy red lips, the drawing reminded Jeff of those old Warner Brothers cartoons where Bugs Bunny dressed in drag, but this particular bunny had size double-D breasts. The cartoon sat atop a Bunny Hop Ranch logo, kicking up its black stiletto heels. Off to the side, a tagline read: "Heaven is just a jump away."

Brooke giggled. "How's that for a sign?"

A turn of the wheel took them onto the side road, the glow of the neon arrow transforming the sands into a Martian landscape.

"They've made the whole desert a red-light district," Jeff said with a laugh, keeping his eyes forward. It was hard to tell where the road stopped and the desert began.

"I think they use red because it's the color of the heart." Her voice was breathy, the way she talked when she was touching herself, trying to get him in the mood. "Red is the color of *passion*."

"DOES SHE WANT TO LEAVE ME FOR SOMEONE ELSE?"

He was about to look over at her, to see if she had her hands in her shorts, but then he saw the house.

Roman columns lined a long, plantation-style porch. Wings branched off from either side of the main house like open arms, each covered in windows, making it appear as if there were a hundred rooms within. White-painted walls were bathed in the glow of spotlights, granting it the appearance of a country inn or house of worship, not a den of sin.

"Wow," he said. "Check this place out."

Brooke reached across the seat for his hand. "Do I have good taste, or what?"

Jeff gave her fingers a light squeeze, his heart beating quicker within his chest. This was it. They were actually going to do this.

Half a dozen cars and trucks sat parked in the sand beside the house. He steered the Durango over to join them, then turned to his wife, taking in her beauty.

"You ready?" he asked.

"Oh yeah." She leaned forward, kissing him softly. "*You're* going to enjoy it, aren't you?"

"I enjoy anything that makes you happy, Brooke," he told her.

"I want to make you happy too." She smiled lovingly, kissing him again even as her hand went to the door.

They started toward the entrance, walking hand-in-hand. Jeff's eyes ran from window to window. Some were dark, others lit, but all had thick, drawn drapes that barred any glimpse of the interior.

"You know," Brooke said, "when I was in college, I thought about working in a brothel."

He tried to sound shocked, "Really?"

"Sure," she confirmed. "I mean, here I was, the only state where it's actually legal to have sex all day long and get paid for it. Talk about your dream job."

The joy in her voice made his stomach sink. "Why didn't you?"

"I fell in love," she told him, then laid her head on his shoulder as they walked. "And I knew I wanted to be with you forever."

Jeff wished he could believe her.

A beautiful Asian girl sat behind a desk in the foyer, her nose in a book titled *Chocolate Park*. Jeff had a thing for Asian girls. His eyes traveled over her flaxen skin and down the inky tresses that pooled on her shoulders. For a moment, he considered asking her if *she* was available for their party, but he quickly thought better of it. She could've been hired solely to answer phones and greet guests, and insinuating that she was a whore might just get him smacked. Besides, Brooke had her heart set on this Xilomen.

You're here for her, remember, not you. For her.

"Excuse me," he said.

The Asian girl stopped reading and smiled. "Welcome to The Ranch. I'm Tanya. How can I help you?"

"We booked a 'couple's party'."

"Very nice." Tanya set her book aside, turning her attention to a large day planner that lay open on the desk. "Name?"

"Kendall."

"You booked Xilomen." A knowing grin bloomed on her lips. She picked up a phone; put it to her ear. "I'll call her down for you."

On the wall behind the desk hung a large sign with the heading "Sexual Menu." Below the title, various sex acts and services were described in great detail, as if each was a meal to be savored in some fancy restaurant. And just like a fine bill of fare, there were no prices.

"Do you know how much this party will cost?" Jeff asked.

Tanya put her hand over the receiver. "Sorry. All the girls are independent contractors. You'll have to negotiate that with—" She uncovered the phone, said, "The Kendalls are here for you," then hung up and looked at him. "She'll be right down. Is this your first time to party with us?"

He snickered. "That obvious, huh?"

"Don't worry," the receptionist assured them as she sat back and reached for her book. "Xilo's the best. She'll take good care of you."

"Now you've done it, Tanya," a voice called out, turning Jeff's head.

A tall, bronze-skinned woman descended a spiral staircase, joining them on the floor of the tiled lobby. Dark brown locks cascaded over her shoulders and down her back, ending at the slender waist of a tight, black dress that showcased her figure. It was a body that promised a night he would never forget.

"You've built up their expectations," she said with a hint of accent. "Now they can't help but be disappointed with me."

Brooke looked at Jeff and laughed. "Judging by the way my husband's mouth is hanging open, I don't think you have anything to worry about."

He noticed an odd tone to his wife's voice, almost like jealousy, but her grin said otherwise.

Their date's smile widened, her dazzling teeth sparkling like pearls between the rose petals of her lips. She slinked over, her long, slender legs ending in black stilettos. "I'm Xilomen, but please, call me Xilo—like J-Lo, but with a Z."

When she slipped her arm in his and escorted them down a hall, Jeff heard chains rattle and slap against wood. His eyes rose to the ceiling. "What was that?"

"One of the girls is entertaining upstairs," Xilo told them matter-of-factly. "Some of our clients enjoy a little bondage."

"Jeff likes it when I tie *him* up," Brooke announced.

"Reeeally?" Xilo flashed a demure grin. "Well, we'll have to see what we can do about that."

He glanced back at his wife, shocked that she would share such an intimate detail, but then he thought, *Relax, you're both gonna fuck this girl in a minute.*

Xilomen opened a door to her left and motioned for them to enter.

According to their website, the ranch had various party suites, each decorated according to its own theme. Jeff had liked the marble columns and statuary of Roman Holiday, but Brooke wanted to party in Paradise Cove.

"It reminds me of our honeymoon in Cancun," she'd told him.

This room, however, was no larger than a walk-in closet. Red drapes hung from floor to ceiling on all four walls, and a tiny security camera was mounted near the ceiling in the corner. Xilo closed the door behind them and stood with her back to the lens.

"I hate talking money," she said. "I much prefer pleasure, which is why we get all that pesky business stuff out of the way up front, so we can move on to..." Her gaze lowered to the crotch of Jeff's jeans. "...bigger and better things."

Brooke smiled at her husband. "And believe me, you won't be disappointed there."

Jeff chuckled; glad to hear Brooke was happy with his manhood.

See, you satisfy her. She's not going to leave you for this woman or anybody else. Stop your worrying and just enjoy yourself. This is The Fantasy, man!

"So..." Xilo's eyes rose to meet his. "How much were you thinking of spending with me tonight?"

He shrugged. "I don't know... the suite, and...everything else. Will five hundred cover it?"

Xilo giggled, then held up her hand and cleared her throat. "I'm sorry, I didn't mean to laugh, I know this is your first time." She pointed to the video camera behind her. "See, that's 'The House.' They're watching to see how much our little party is going to make for them. They get half of everything we earn here. So, if I took five hundred from you, I'd only really earn two-fifty."

Jeff looked into the lens, his stomach fluttering. "You need a thousand?"

She smiled sweetly. "If you triple that, I think we can have a real nice party."

"*Three* thousand?" Maybe he'd seen too many movies or *Law & Order* episodes, where the hookers charged guys twenty bucks for a blow job, but he wasn't expecting anything close to that amount. "Is that for the whole night?"

"It would be for a few hours. To have me overnight, wow, that would be close to five figures."

Jeff's eyes widened and shot to Brooke.

"Relax," his wife told him, reaching into her purse. "You take Visa and Mastercard, don't you?"

Xilo nodded. "American Express too."

Jeff grabbed Brooke's arm. "Hon, you can't be serious."

"Don't worry." She gave his hand a gentle squeeze. "My card, my treat."

Paradise Cove featured faux-bamboo walls, an imitation palm-thatched ceiling, and painted windows that opened onto a painted sea. In the corner, silk ferns and palms surrounded a huge, kidney-shaped tub, forming a secluded rainforest grotto.

Jeff took off his watch and shoes. "So how long have you worked here?"

Xilomen chuckled as she drew a bath. "You mean how long have I been a whore?"

His face warmed. "Okay, yeah."

"A long time." She kicked off her heels and sat on the edge of the tub, moving her hand through the water to check the temperature, her reflection riding the ripples.

"Well, how long have you been in the U.S.?"

"I've been here for many years. The people who took control of my country..." Her face clouded over for a moment. "There was torture, persecution, but my mother saved me and brought me here for a better life."

Jeff nodded, wondering if selling her body night after night was the "better life" Xilo's mother had envisioned. He took off his shirt and tossed it onto a wicker chair in the corner, sweat beading on his chest, back and forehead. It could've been nerves, but he thought it was more likely the Viagra. Xilo had offered it to him, and he'd taken it gladly, wanting to make certain they got their money's worth.

Brooke unbuttoned her blouse. The butterfly etched on her left breast looked as if it were trying to escape the jaws of the winged serpent at her hip.

Xilo saw the markings and smiled. "*Cihuacoatl*."

Jeff didn't speak Spanish. "Excuse me?"

His wife snickered and her hands went to her pantyline, stretching her skin to flatten the artwork. "She's talking about my tattoo. It's *Cihuacoatl*, the Aztec serpent goddess, 'mother of humanity'."

"That's right." Xilo sounded impressed. "But She didn't create us all at once. Women were formed first. Men came much later, made from *tonalli*, the blood of the womb."

Jeff gave his wife's new body art more scrutiny. She'd never told him the meaning behind it, only that she thought it was cool.

Xilo shut off the faucet, then moved toward Brooke. Minus their heels, they were the same height, no taller than Jeff's chin. "You know, during certain rituals, the women who worshiped *Cihuacoatl* would explore each other... sexually."

She leaned in, hesitated; when she saw that Brooke did not shy away, she kissed her. It began as a gentle peck, then grew in intensity, their tongues probing each other's mouths with great enthusiasm.

As Jeff sat there, hypnotized by desire, his jeans grew tight. He tugged at the zipper and quickly shed them, liberating his erection.

"Why haven't I heard about this religion?" Brooke asked, a string of saliva still tethering her lips to Xilo's. "I would've signed up years ago."

"SHE COMES FORTH, PLUMED WITH FEATHERS, PAINTED WITH BLOOD..."

"Spanish Conquistadors found homosexuality evil." Xilo reached up and undid the clasps of Brooke's bra, sliding the straps off her shoulders and down her arms.

"They took the followers of *Cihuacoatl*, staked them to the ground, and set them on fire. Later, Jesuits destroyed the Aztec libraries, trying to eradicate any hint that they ever existed. Even today, the government of Peru destroys any pottery it unearths with same-sex images. They say it 'insults their national honor'."

Xilo lowered her head to Brooke's perky, rose-tipped breast, tracing the butterfly marking with her tongue.

"You never see a woman with a caterpillar tattoo," she said between licks. "Caterpillars are ugly. They do nothing but eat, sleep, and fight with one another. But then the creator steps in, as if to correct a mistake, and they are transformed, they turn into something truly wonderful, and then all women want them."

Jeff saw Brooke shut her eyes, chewing her lower lip as Xilo's mouth closed around the firm nub of her nipple. It was the same face she made when *he* worked on her breasts, and now, to see her get identical satisfaction from the touch of a woman filled him with an odd brew of envy and excitement.

When Brooke opened her eyes again, she looked at him and smiled. "I think my husband needs some attention."

Xilomen stood and took Brooke by the hand, offering Jeff a lascivious grin. "I know just the thing."

They walked over to the bedside table. Xilo opened the drawer and took out a handful of scarves. "You take his hands; I'll do his feet."

Brooke giggled. She took hold of Jeff's wrist and wrapped it in sheer fabric.

He frowned and pulled away. "I don't know if I feel comfortable—"

"Pleeeease," his wife begged. "Do it for me."

Give her what she wants, buddy. You don't want her to

leave you.

He reluctantly offered up his hand again.

"Now lay down," Brooke instructed.

Jeff did as he was told, allowing the women to lash his limbs to the bedframe. Xilo hummed as she tightened the knots, and he lifted his head to look at her. "What's that?"

"Oh, we were talking about *Cihuacoatl*, and I remembered a hymn my mother taught me." She cleared her throat, then sang, "*She comes forth, plumed with feathers, painted with blood, She is our mother, a goddess of war, our mother a goddess of war...*"

"You've got a great voice," Brooke told her, finishing the last of the knots.

Xilo smiled, then reached up and slid the spaghetti straps from her shoulders, allowing her black dress to fall to the floor. Her naked body surpassed even Jeff's wildest expectations. She motioned for Brooke to join her at the foot of the bed, and the two women knelt on either side of him, exchanging a playful glance across his erection before bringing it to their soft, full lips.

Jeff relaxed, let his arms and legs hang, let his head fall back against the satin pillow, and concentrated on the feel of warm, wet mouths; the gorgeous friction of their fingers as they massaged his length. Even with his eyes pinched shut he could tell who was who. The metal stud of Brooke's piercing raked and tickled his most sensitive flesh; the tip of Xilo's tongue slithered its way up his shaft in a serpentine motion.

And then they stopped.

He opened his eyes and looked down the length of the bed as Xilomen climbed onto him. She positioned herself over his erection, then sank onto his lap. As he slid deep into the moist shadows between her legs, Jeff groaned with pleasure, then realized he wasn't wearing a condom.

Before he could say anything, Brooke straddled his face. She grabbed the headboard and pressed herself against his open mouth until her pubic bone flattened his nose. Thick fluid bathed his tongue in a sudden glut. It was warm, salty.

Blood!

It ran down the back of Jeff's throat, gagging him.

He squirmed, and kicked; his bonds snapped taught and strangled his wrists and ankles, but his wife seemed not to notice. She seized him by the hair and held him down with her weight.

Does she know I can't breathe?

his shocked brain wondered. *I'm drowning, drowning in blood!*

Suddenly, as if she'd heard his thoughts, Brooke released her grip and rolled off his face, scarlet tears staining her milky inner thighs.

She was smiling.

Jeff coughed up rosy spittle. It rained into his eyes and ran from the corners of his mouth as he tried to draw breath. "What the... blood!"

"*Tonalli,*" Xilo corrected, mounting him as if nothing had happened. She placed her palms on his chest and leaned in, her body moving up and down, her eyes locking with his as she spoke. "It is the 'animating spirit.' Without it, everything stops. There can be no joy without blood. No love. No future. No *life.*"

Brooke gave Xilo a long, passionate kiss, then knelt beside the bed, her fingers combing Jeff's sweaty hair. "It's okay, baby," she told him. "She'll be here soon. It's going to be wonderful, you'll see."

Jeff stared at his wife, uncomprehending. He pulled on his restraints to no avail, then turned his attention to the woman on his lap. "Get off me, you sick bitch! Let me up!"

"When we're finished," Xilomen assured him, moving her hips, making his penetrations deeper and even more silken.

"*Now!*"

Xilo ignored him. She closed her eyes and continued to ride him as she sang the rest of *Cihuacoatl*'s hymn, "*She comes forth, She appears when war is waged, She protects us in war, that we shall not be destroyed, that we shall never be parted...*"

The door creaked open and someone entered the room. Jeff strained his neck to see who it was and caught a glimpse of rainbow feathers, just like Brooke's tattoo.

It can't be...

He glared at his wife, her menstrual blood cooling on his lips as he screamed, "*Untie me!*"

She ran her fingers through his hair, but said nothing.

He heard a long hiss, like a slashed tire breathing its last. His heart hammered and he frantically pulled at his bonds, rattling the bedframe. "*Brooke!*"

"We're saving you," she told him, her voice calm and loving, her eyes aglow. "Now I'll never lose you. We'll be together forever."

The blue pill continued to work its magic, keeping Jeff's cock an iron rod in spite of his fear, and Xilomen impaled herself upon it again and again, chanting, "*She comes adorned in the ancient manner, plumed with feathers... plumed with...feathers...*"

Brooke looked up and smiled with excitement. "She's here."

Jeff turned his head, following his wife's line of sight, and his gaze was met by reptilian eyes the size of footballs. Bright peacock quills crowned the serpent's forehead, and long, slender arms hung from its sides. Its thin, scaly lips peeled back, revealing fangs like walrus tusks. His body tensed, expecting the animal to strike. Instead, it kept its distance, its massive head swaying back and forth, holding Jeff in its gaze as if Brooke and Xilo were not even in the room.

A rattlesnake's jangle filled the air, providing music for Xilo's lyrics.

"*She comes forth,*" she crooned, breathing harder, her hips moving faster, "*our mother, a goddess...*"

Jeff's mouth was dry, mute. He closed his eyes, hoping that this was just a nightmare, that his fear of losing his wife had finally pulled him over the edge, dragging him down into an abyss of madness.

"*She comes forth, She comes... She comes...*" Xilomen cried out in ecstasy, and Jeff's eyes sprang open to stare into the gutted sockets of a charred skull. The young beauty from the Internet was gone, replaced by a seared corpse that was somehow able to move. Her scorched hand reached down, her brittle fingers caressing his cheek. The blackened, leathery skin around her teeth pulled back to form a grotesque grin, and she finished her song, "*...to make you an example and a companion.*"

Jeff tried to scream, but all he could manage was a dry, cracked whine. He tilted his head toward Brooke, but his wife didn't seem the least bit shocked. Either she couldn't see the ghoul that mounted him, or she'd seen it before.

Cihuacoatl rattled and hissed, and the cacophony became deafening. It reached out, its claw touching his chest, the hot fingers sinking into his flesh as if it were butter. He felt his bones crack and expand, felt the skin come loose from its moorings and drift across his body, congealing into odd, alien formations, and then the room was bathed in blinding blue light.

Brooke climbed the stairs. Her last client had been overweight, hairy, more ape than human being, and he came far too quickly. At least his money had been good.

Now what she needed was a *real* man.

Before bringing Jeff here to the ranch, she'd been afraid he would leave her. She wasn't blind. She noticed the way he looked at other women, especially Asian women, and in her mind, she saw him having affairs with girls who were taller, younger, thinner, or just more exotic-looking than she was. And when they arrived here that first night, when her husband saw Tanya, the receptionist, and undressed her with his eyes, she knew she'd made the right decision.

Brooke had originally looked at a threesome as a way for Jeff to get those fantasies out of his system, a way to share the experience and keep him from going behind her back. The quest to make him happy led her here, to a secret meeting with Xilomen, where she learned the truth of *Cihuacoatl*'s power and was shown the promise of eternal life, of youth and beauty long after death. Now they would always be together, and she would have her husband's love for all time.

Thank the goddess for saving our marriage, for saving us!

She opened the door to her room, but left the light off. "Jeff?"

His eyes shone like twin lamps, illuminating the darkened corner. Buds of sinew flapped and waved along his sides, and the chain that hung from his collar jingled and slapped the wooden floor.

He was excited to see her.

Jeff used his lengthy new appendages to crawl up onto the bed. A long, glistening tongue hung from his mandibles, and a massive erection reached out from his pelvis like a fisted arm.

Brooke licked her lips as she closed the door.

It was all for her.

Michael West is a member of the Horror Writers Association and serves as President of its local chapter, Indiana Horror Writers. His first novel, *The Wide Game*, was published in 2003, and since that time, he has written a multitude of short stories, articles, and reviews for various on-line and print publications. A graduate of Indiana University, West has a degree in Telecommunications and Film Theory. He lives and works in the Indianapolis area with his wife, their two children, their bird, Rodan, and turtle, Gamera.

His children are convinced that spirits move through the woods near their home.

Find more from Michael at *bymichaelwest.com*.

Daniel R. Robichaud
Fritz Lieber: Smoke, Ghosts & Terror

> *"It is the American metropolis, jammed with iron and stone, that sets off my sense of the horrible—[...] Things like the buzz of a defective neon sign, the black framework of the elevated, the muttering of machinery one cannot identify—there are terrors in the modern city in comparison to which the darks of Gothic castles and haunted woods are light!"*[1]

Though he is perhaps best known for introducing the world to the memorable sword and sorcery duo Fafhrd and the Gray Mouser, Fritz Leiber's storytelling skills were in no way limited to the field of heroic fantasy. Leiber helped pave the way for modern horror with such tales as *Conjure Wife*, "The Girl with Hungry Eyes" and "Dark Wings." While each of these works is deserving of appreciation, this article concerns one of his earliest stories, a piece that remains remarkable not only for leaving its footprint upon the history of the genre but for its continuing influence.

Readers of Street and Smith's *Unknown* magazine may have been surprised to find the October 1941 issue retitled. What had been simply *Unknown* had become the more science fiction sounding *Unknown Worlds*. What they could not have anticipated was that one of the stories between this particular issue's covers, a macabre piece with the unassuming name of "Smoke Ghost," would not only have a long shelf life but would establish a completely new paradigm for terror fiction. Whereas Lovecraft is rightly attributed as the defining force of cosmic horror, Fritz Leiber's "Smoke Ghost" developed urban horror.[2]

For those as yet unfamiliar with the story, I highly recommend seeking it out. The story has found its way into a variety of outlets over the years. In fact, the notes section following this article includes a few suggestions.

> "IT IS THE AMERICAN METROPOLIS, JAMMED WITH IRON AND STONE, THAT SETS OFF MY SENSE OF THE HORRIBLE..."

As this article's intent is a close examination of the story and its effects, it will deal with the tale in a frank fashion. For those requiring such niceties, let me go on the record and say that "Here follow spoilers aplenty."

You have been warned.

The construction of Leiber's story seems surprisingly simplistic, hiding its complexities within an easily accessible, highly readable text. The action occurs in four major scenes (one a flashback) connected by several brief, atmospheric transition sequences. The story is remarkably bloodless, terrifying through the "quiet" principles of atmosphere and ambience. However, "Smoke Ghost" is by no means a gentle story.

Protagonist Catesby Wran is a haunted man. Not, as he explains to secretary Miss Millick, by anything resembling a traditional ghost, Wran is pursued by

> *"...a ghost from the world today, with the soot of factories on its face and the pounding of machinery in its soul. The kind that would haunt coal yards and slip around at night through deserted office buildings like this one. A real ghost. Not something out of books."*[4]

A subsequent flashback reveals the haunting to be due to a seemingly chance encounter on the elevated train. While looking out the window, Wran becomes aware of an indistinct form on the grimy rooftops of Chicago. After several days, he realizes the form has taken note of him, as well. Attempting to find recourse in two of the three pillars of sanity in the modern day[4], Wran administers a dose of common sense through rationalization (conversing with his secretary) and then visits psychiatrist Dr. Trevethick. Neither of these avenues proves effective in dispelling the phantom, but several key elements do come to light. Wran reveals that he was something of a perhaps paranormally sensitive youth, gifted with the ability of hyper-acute awareness. Not necessarily to the Otherworldly, the young Wran found himself quite attuned to the details of this world and its occupants, "...able to see through walls, read letters through envelopes and books through their covers, fence and play ping-pong blindfolded, find things that were buried, read thoughts."[5] This ability vanished after a traumatic incident in his youth (a pair of university researchers attempted to replicate his abilities in a public forum, but only succeeded in terrifying the child to inability), but is inferred to be responsible for his awareness of the urban spirit.

When these pillars of stability fail to provide relief, Wran finds himself pondering what such a being would desire. An earlier observation, "What would such a thing want from a person, Miss Millick? Sacrifice? Worship? Or just fear?"[6] returns when Wran ultimately finds himself facing the titular being directly. This horror is not the remnant of a human being, but a manifestation of the city itself. To survive, Wran yields it complete subservience. While this sacrifice may buy him some respite, Wran is only too aware of the relentlessness of this presence. This is not a ghost to be dispelled, but simply appeased for a time.

Though representative of the time of its writing, the macabre treasures within "Smoke Ghost" are by no means tarnished with age. The urban environment is still very much with us, and while current cities may seem somewhat different than Leiber's sooty portrayal of 1940s Chicago, there are still plenty of filthy rooftops and claustrophobic corners within any city's boundaries for horror to lurk. The story remains timely and chilling.

Just as the ghost of Leiber's tale seems omnipresent in its urban environment, so too does Leiber's story linger in the horrors written today. Authors who use the urban environment not only as a simple backdrop, but as a source for supernatural terror, reveal the "Smoke Ghost" legacy.

Though its American branch remains somewhat dominated by small town settings, modern horror fiction is no stranger to urban environments. Leiber himself revisited this particular territory in his own *Our Lady of Darkness* (as well as numerous short stories), but leaves plenty of room for others to add to the work.

Over the years, plenty of authors have tackled Leiber's ideas in their own fiction. From a variety of paranoiac personalities (often beset by difficult to discern supernatural presences) in numerous works by Ramsey Campbell, to the subterranean born horrors of T.E.D. Klein's urban nightmare novella, *Children of the Kingdom* (in his *Dark Gods* collection), to Harlan Ellison's chilling meditation

upon the infamous murder of Kitty Genovese in "A Whimper of Whipped Dogs," to Clive Barker's tortured souls in urban hells (exemplified by various stories in the *Books of Blood*, such as "The Midnight Meat Train"), authors still grapple with the spirit (as it were) of Leiber's short story.

However, the influence stems even wider than to a single genre. Outside of straight horror, readers can find "Smoke Ghost" resonance in everything from Neil Gaiman's run on *Sandman*[7], to China Mieville's New Crobuzon in *Perdido Street Station*, to John Shirley's literal portrayal of city as character in his ur-cyberpunk novel *City Come A-Walkin'*.

Like ripples in a disturbed pool, the echoes of "Smoke Ghost" can also be found much further afield than American or European genre fiction. How can one read about the origins of Sadako Yamamura, the psychically endowed antagonist of Koji Suzuki's *Ringu*, without then considering the young Catesby Wran's sensitivity and testing traumas? Both Wran and Sadako are cut from a similar cloth, though their respective characters venture in very different directions. Then again, it is not a terrible stretch to suggest that Sadako's posthumous fate—"haunting" a videotape and promising death to any who watch it, should they not make the proper sacrifices—is to become her own smoke ghost.

Can one read about the haunted, crumbling apartment complex of Koji Suzuki's "Floating Water" (filmed in both Japan and America as *Dark Water*), where taps offer water thick with "countless particles of dirt"[8] without recalling the disintegrating haunts and sooty spoor of Leiber's composite faced ghost?

Certainly readers can ignore the roots of fiction, as each of these mentioned works stands quite well on its own. However, while the stories are each individually interesting, when taken as components to a larger literary dialogue, they fascinate and provoke on wholly different levels. Whether the authors are actively engaging Leiber's story or simply drawing upon the elements that have found their way into the cultural milieu, each author brings new insights and perspective to what has come before.

Of course, "Smoke Ghost" did not appear whole cloth and without literary antecedents. Leiber drew upon a rich history of terror fiction, at once reviving "the reticence of M.R. James in contemporary fashion"[9] and serving up the "descendent of the stories of other dimensions such as Blackwood's 'The Willows' or Bierce's 'The Damned Thing' or Frank Belknap Long's 'The Hounds of Tindalos',"[10] making this dialogue rich with the history of the genre.

"Smoke Ghost" has proven to be a robust story, and a fine springboard for both nightmares and new fiction. I have no doubt it will continue to affect, stimulate and influence whole new generations of readers and writers.

Daniel R. Robichaud grew up in Michigan, and attended college at Oakland University in Rochester Hills, Michigan. He somehow managed to earn himself Degrees in Physics and English, and even an M.A. in English.

He is happily married and currently living in Worcester, Mass., where by day he slaves as a research engineer. By night, he's a writer. Somewhere in between, he tries to be a good husband.

Daniel is assistant editor for *horrorreader.com*, and his short stories have appeared in numerous magazines and anthologies. For more on Daniel's current works, stop by *home.earthlink.net/~dtrobichaud2*.

Notes

1. Fritz Leiber, *Night's Black Agents* (Berkley Medallion Books, 1978), i. The full quotation includes specific references to aspects of the city as related in such stories as "The Inheritance," "Diary in the Snow," and (of course) "Smoke Ghost."

2. One anthology (long out of print, unfortunately) that includes Leiber's story is *Urban Horrors*, edited by William F. Nolan and Martin H. Greenberg (Daw Books, 1993). This volume—collecting short stories dealing with urban set horror from a variety of authors, including Shirley Jackson, John Cheever, Joyce Carol Oates, Ray Bradbury, Richard Matheson and Joe R. Lansdale—includes Leiber's seminal work as its first selection. The brief introduction to the volume suggests that while urban horror has

"extended roots" (applying the label to Robert Louis Stevenson's *Strange Case of Dr Jekyll and Mr Hyde*), not until Leiber's fiction was urban horror "recognized as a separate subgenre within the literature of terror." (pg. 1) While the actual notion of urban horror being a full-fledged subgenre is debatable, the editors are correct in their observation that prior to Leiber's story, the urban environment never played such a vital role in terror fiction.

3. Leiber, *Night's Black Agents*, 109.

4. Ibid, 111. When confronted with his secretary's observation that ghosts do not, in fact, exist, Wran responds with a condescending affirmative, adding that "Science and common sense and psychiatry all go to prove it." This trio represents the three aspects of modern society's attempts to explain away the supernatural.

5. Ibid., 116.

6. Ibid., 110.

7. In particular, Gaiman's story "A Tale of Two Cities," which appeared in the World's End arc of *Sandman* (DC Comics, Issue 51), follows a protagonist drawn into a nightmarish sequence which ends with the startling realization that he has fallen into the dream of the city itself and a chilling consideration about what might happen should the City rouse from its slumber.

8. Koji Suzuki, *Dark Water* (Vertical, 2004), 15. While the story is ultimately concerned with a more traditional sort of ghost—a vanished young girl's spirit haunts the flat of an unrelated, single mother protagonist—the urban environment plays no small role in the tale. In fact, the building is erected upon a landfill, a foundation of "the dregs of several generations." (pg 16).

9. Ramsey Campbell, "Fritz Leiber," *The Irish Journal of Gothic and Horror Studies,* Lost Souls webpage. http://irishgothichorrorjournal.homestead.com/lostsouls.html#anchor_148.

10. *The Dark Descent III: A Fabulous Formless Darkness* (Tor Books, 1987), 17. An anthology of horror fiction which includes the story as its first offering. Editor David G. Hartwell's introduction further notes that "The impact of this story on horror writing in the U.S. can scarcely be overestimated. It is a revolutionary ghost story that rethinks the entire tradition and re-imagines the supernatural in our time." As of this writing, Tor Books recently republished *The Dark Descent* as an omnibus volume.

Acknowledgements: Thank you to Ramsey Campbell for sending me a copy of his "Fritz Leiber" article. Thanks also to David Read, webmaster of Fritz Leiber's official website, for additional information.

DARK REGIONS BOOKS
PUBLISHERS OF FINE HORROR, FANTASY, AND SCIENCE FICTION

SHADOWS AND OTHER TALES
BY TONY RICHARDS
LETTERED EDITION
$150

100 SIGNED LIMITED HARDCOVER ED. $45
THIS AD ONLY $35

SIGNED TRADE PAPERBACK $19.95
THIS AD ONLY $16.95

ENNUI AND OTHER STATES OF MADNESS
BY DAVID NIALL WILSON
LETTERED EDITION
$150

100 SIGNED LIMITED HARDCOVER ED. $50
THIS AD ONLY $40

SIGNED TRADE PAPERBACK $19.95
THIS AD ONLY $16.95

OTHER GODS
BY STEPHEN MARK RAINEY
LETTERED EDITION
$150

100 SIGNED LIMITED HARDCOVER ED. $45
THIS AD ONLY $35

SIGNED TRADE PAPERBACK $19.95
THIS AD ONLY $16.95

WINGS
BY SARAH A. HOYT
LETTERED EDITION
$125

SIGNED TRADE PAPERBACK $18.95
THIS AD ONLY $15.95

THE NIGHTMARE COLLECTION
BY BRUCE BOSTON
TRADE PAPERBACK POETRY COLLECTION
$9.95
THIS AD ONLY $7.95

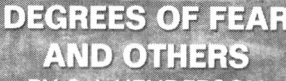

DEGREES OF FEAR AND OTHERS
BY C.J. HENDERSON
LETTERED EDITION
$125

100 SIGNED LIMITED HARDCOVER ED. $45
THIS AD ONLY $35

SIGNED TRADE PAPERBACK $18.95
THIS AD ONLY $16.95

• FREE USPS MEDIA SHIPPING •

SHADOWS & OTHER TALES:
☐ LETTERED $150 ☐ HARDCOVER $35 ☐ PAPERBACK $16.95 _____

ENNUI & OTHER STATES OF MADNESS:
☐ LETTERED $150 ☐ HARDCOVER $40 ☐ PAPERBACK $16.95 _____

OTHER GODS:
☐ LETTERED $150 ☐ HARDCOVER $45 ☐ PAPERBACK $16.95 _____

WINGS:
☐ LETTERED $125 ☐ PAPERBACK $15.95 _____

THE NIGHTMARE COLLECTION:
☐ PAPERBACK $7.95 _____

DEGREES OF FEAR AND OTHERS:
☐ LETTERED $125 ☐ HARDCOVER $35 ☐ PAPERBACK $16.95 _____

TOTAL: _____

FOR FURTHER INFORMATION VISIT WWW.DARKREGIONS.COM

NAME: _____
ADDRESS: _____
ADDRESS: _____
CITY, ST, ZIP: _____
PHONE: _____
EMAIL: _____

The Hiram Grange Chronicles

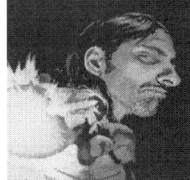

Excerpt from...

Hiram Grange & the Twelve Little Hitlers

Scott Christian Carr

Jodie. Always, there is Jodie...

Hiram types furiously, fingers dancing over the grime-encrusted keys of his ancient laptop. Burnt-out pixels, sticky trackball mouse. Dial-up—his connection to the larger world is slow, but intoxicating.

You're tied up, he types. *I'm tickling you with a feather. Starting with your toes. Moving up... up... UP!!!*

LOL! replies **jfoster222**. In another window, **FBI-Clarice** writes, *I'm licking my lips, licking your hard, hairy chest... your rock-solid abs...*

My 6-pack, types Hiram. (Never mind his bony ribcage—the gaunt, doughy gut nestled beneath his loosened tie and unbuttoned buttons, sweat-stained shirt, tweed jacket. Shirttails dangling over khaki trousers. Fly unzipped.) He pushes his spectacles further up the bridge of his sweaty, uneven nose. The anticipation is rising. In another window **Jodierocks** writes, *I want you so bad!*

From the radio blares a techno-remix of the Violent *Femmes* perennial classic:

Why can't I get just one kiss?
Why can't I get just one kiss?

Hiram spares a glance at the Mission Oak chair in the corner of his dusty, tobacco-infused study. Blue wisps of Presbyterian tobacco smoke drift lazily to the ceiling. The opium infused tobacco burns his lungs, gives his vision a fuzzy, fiery frame. He regards the antique chair coolly, licking his swollen, oversized fish-lips. In it now, a schoolgirl. Plaid and pretty. Bound and gagged. Tied securely—she bats her long lashes provocatively at him and screams *Do me! Do me! Do me!* with her eyes.

Believe me, some things I wouldn't miss...

Hiram blinks. The wave of weirdness washes over him and he swigs another gulp of *Glenfiddich* to straighten his brain. Straight from the bottle, washing the acrid bite of leftover pills from under his tongue and down his throat, replacing bitterness with fire.

He's headed for a dark place—the roller coaster is nearing the top of its run, and it's soon to be a long, hard fall for Hiram Grange... a long fall and loop-de-loop. But he'll pull out just before hitting rock bottom. He always does...

But for now, the Binge.

But I look at your pants and... I NEED a Kiss!

He shakes another pill onto his palm and wags his tongue at the Mission Oak chair—now seating not a schoolgirl but a cheerleader. Not tied, but slouched. Legs splayed in a suggestive rendition of Sharon Stone's *Basic Instinct* striptease.

Hiram swallows the pill and turns his attention back to the computer. His focus is starting to waver. Reality is starting to splinter. Message windows blur, double—keyboard keys dance and trade places. *I'm fliping you over*, Hiram types, never missing the missing "P"—*I'm pushing your face down into the pillow.* And then, in a moment of stoned inspiration, he types, *Are your lambs screaming yet???*

A crash from the bathroom. Breaking glass and a muffled yell. Muted behind the deadlocked door. Hiram pays it no mind. He's on a roll, he's in the zone, he's beyond the point of turning back...

Another message window. This one from **Gashleycrumb**. The message is entirely written in Cyrillic.

Хаве military фоунд тхем сет?

Hiram tells **jfoster222** that he's naked now. That he's harder than he's ever been.

In the Mission Oak now, a naughty nurse.

Gashleycrumb persists: *Хас хе талкед?*

He warns **Jodierocks** to get ready, that he might, just might, be too big for her…

Gashleycrumb replies immediately and in English. *Hiram? Too big? Is that code? What happened to Cyrillic?*

Hiram's hit the wall. Cyber-coitus interruptus. Faux pas. Bad move. Major fuck-up.

Sorry, his long fingers dance over the keys. *Wrong window.*

The Mission Oak, empty now. Naked embarrassment temporarily clearing his mind of fevered hallucination.

More muffled grunts from the bathroom.

Gashleycrumb responds with a series of question marks, capped with an exclamation point.

Rubbing his eyes, Hiram pulls a small chalkboard closer to him on the desk. He tries to focus, begins scribbling furiously. The Cyrillic was his idea. He writes feverishly, decoding **Gashleycrumb's** message. *Хаве соу фоунд тхем сем? Have you found any of the others yet?*

Not yet, he types. Better to keep it short.

He pops another pill. Takes another drink. *Take off the edge, focus…*

Cyrillic chicken-scratch fills the chalkboard, as he continues to translate.

Хас хе талкед? Has he talked?

Hiram rubs his boney chin and considers his reply. For a long moment he regards the deadlocked bathroom door. The grunting has stopped, but he can still hear muffled movement from inside.

Working on it, he types. Hits "REPLY." Slams the laptop lid shut. And then, like a cat he's out of his seat and at the bathroom door—silently and in the blink of an eye. He has a hammer in his hand.

In a blur of motion he throws open the lock, kicks ajar the door and reaches in. Betraying a strength that one would think impossible in such a scrawny frame, he fishes out a man by the scruff of his shirt, whirls him around and pushes, half-throws, him into the room. The young man staggers backwards, falling into the Mission Oak.

Hiram pounces. Raises the hammer menacingly. When the boy (for in the harsh lamplight of the study we can see that his terrified face betrays little more than peach-fuzz, and the beginnings of a paintbrush mustache on his trembling upper lip) begins to speak, Hiram raises a finger to his own lips, shushing him.

"Not a word," hisses Grange. "I don't want you to talk. I want you to *think* about talking. Think about what you're *going to say*. Think about telling me where your brothers are. And don't even think about giving me a snow job. Even without the mustache, I know who you are. Whose cloth you're cut from, as it were." Hiram raises the hammer as if to strike. "I'll be right back. We're not gonna move now, are we?" The boy shakes his head.

"Good," says Hiram, stepping into the small library (a cramped room that, until recently, served the current, vacationing owners of the apartment as a food pantry). From the shelf he pulls *The Collected Works of Lewis Carroll*. It's a thick book, musty with antiquity, and a perfectly-sized hiding place of cut-out pages and secret compartment. From inside its covers Hiram removes a plastic ziplocked baggie. From it he pours a handful of red-capped *Amanita muscaria*—psychedelic faerie mushrooms, and of a particularly potent strain.

He places the book back on its shelf. Then, after a moment's consideration, he removes a copy of *Mein Kampf* and tucks it under his arm. He might need to refer to it—at the very least, it was heavy enough that he might be able to bludgeon the clone in the Mission Oak chair with it, without doing any permanent damage before he could answer all of the questions that needed answering.

Hiram takes a deep breath, steadies his nerves, and swallows a handful of the scarlet mushrooms. After all, no one should have to confront Hitler straight.

Hitler is crying. Blubbering like a baby. Weeping, tears streaming from innocent eyes, mustache wet with snot, jowls jiggling with each sob—bawling.

He looks more like an overgrown toddler, a spoiled brat, a trust fund ne'er-do-well—than the teenage monster that he is.

"I didn't do nothin', man," his voice cracks. "Please…"

"The hell you didn't," Hiram levels the book at him. Makes as if to strike, then tosses it into his lap. The splayed pages of *Mein Kampf* blurred by Hitler's tears and dripping snot. All but unreadable.

The single malt psychedelia starts to kick in strong. It's a dangerous dementia. A bad mix. A sweaty, fevered, cold-blooded mean kinda trip. Uncontrollable. Hiram begins to shake. Can't stop sweating. Tries to speak but can't. Fists clenching and unclenching at his sides. Hammer drops to the floor.

Hitler tries to get up, tries to escape.

With a detached derring-do, faster than fast, Hiram pulls his piece.

His father's gun: Hitler's mouth.

.455 caliber *Webley*.

Squeeze — don't pull — squeeeezzzzze… and…

Click.

Hitler slumps back into his chair. Shaking, trembling, sobbing.

I made Hitler cry, Hiram thinks. *I'm making Hitler cry!*

Hiram is shaking for the worse now. Sweat is pouring down his face, stinging his eyes, dripping from his chin. He's paler even than usual. He reaches up and wipes his brow and flips the switch on the cord of the recently installed *Mole-Richardson Baby-Senior Solarspot*. A theatre lamp he'd rescued from the dumpster in the alley behind *The Regalia Improv*

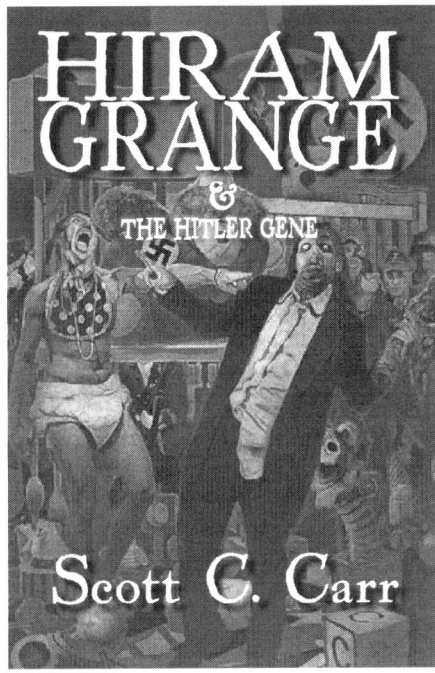

next door. Illegal for indoor home use. 5,000 watts. At three feet it can blind anyone insane enough to open their eyes. At three feet, in just 10 minutes, it will cook the skin off of a chicken.

Hiram flips the switch and Hitler is bathed in unrelenting light, an unwilling angel with an unholy halo. Hiram is hidden in shadow, the diffuser clips and anodized aluminum bouncing the light away from him and onto Hitler.

"In 1938," Hiram declares, "Hitler was voted *Time Magazine's* Man of the Year." No response from the impenetrable hot glow enveloping the Mission Oak. "Before World War Two the New York phone book had twenty-two Hitlers. After World War Two, it had none." Still no response.

"*Can you hear me!*" Hiram screams. The waves of euphoric insanity are coming faster now, harder. "*Are you alive?*" he demands.

"Turn it off!" Hitler screams. Already, the temperature in the room has climbed ten degrees. "It's burning!"

Instead, Hiram drops the needle of the *Stack-o-Matic* and fills the room with the amplified earsplitting melodies of Bach's *Toccata and Fugue*, to accompany the blinding glare of the lamp. Much louder here than on his antique Victrola back home…

…and for a moment Hiram is swept away in an undercurrent of psychotropic nostalgia—fond thoughts of his old *Airstream* RV. Alone and abandoned. Off-limits. Unsafe. *Being watched*. With a sharp crackle of brain-lightning and the smell of ozone in his nostrils and the musky taste of spores on his tongue, Hiram's fanciful nostalgia is, just like that, ripped away by an undertow of paranoid fury. How *dare* they drive him away from his home—whoever they are! How dare they force him to break into and squat (unbeknownst to its owners) in this fabulous and fully-furnished upscale apartment? Hiding like a mouse. Like a rat. Like a criminal…

He'll find them, those watchers, and he'll kill them. Kill 'em all. Murder every last one of the bastards. Whoever they are. Just as soon as he's completed the mission.

The mission… The mission… His mind is racing, clouded and flowing like melting Jell-O, molten lava. *Mission? Just what is the mission, exactly?*

Hitler is screaming now. Begging for mercy… The squeaky sing-song warble of Gordon Gano and the *Violent Femmes* tries to compete, but is all but lost in the myriad textures of Bach and the terrified and painful death throes of Little H. It's hot as hell in the apartment and Hiram can smell the thick, oily stench of smoldering hair. His stomach growls.

Rumbles of desperate, unacknowledged hunger.

He hasn't eaten in days. Can't keep anything down. The hunger is there—but it's overshadowed by the nausea of the mind-candy. The mushrooms. The opium. The tobacco, alcohol and wine. There's a subtle, atavistic craving for curry, for the nuclear fury of the Naga Jolokia pepper, the exotic spices of the Orient—for razor clams, for savory chilled abalone, for takiyaki octopus balls… But then, drowning it all, there is *The Binge*.

Starving, Hiram knows that he couldn't keep any food in his stomach, not if his life depended on it. The mushrooms wouldn't let him. The opium wouldn't let him. The pills and *Glenfiddich* wouldn't let him.

The smell of smoldering Hitler wouldn't let him.

There'll be plenty of time to gorge himself later, he tells himself, plenty of time for fine dining, for compulsive cuisine, fast-food take-out and gourmet indulgences… but for now there is only the binge. *The Binge…* and *The Mission*.

Mission? Again, with the mission… What is the mission?

The mission…

The mission is sitting in the Mission Oak chair…

Hitler's middle name was Elizabeth.

The *real* Hitler, that is—no, strike that, the *first* Hitler.

Hitler had only one testicle.

True facts.

Hitler invented the blow-up sex doll.

True fact.

He wanted to keep his soldiers satisfied and not planting their seed in foreign women. Blonde hair, blue eyes. Large

Your Horror Collection Would be in Ruins without Shroud.

Visit Us Today

www.shroudmagazine.com

Books, Magazines, More

breasts, white plastic skin…

Another pang of hunger. Another wave of nausea.

Another blast of crazy.

He'd fed Little Hitler the leftovers of three week old kimchee just that morning—coagulated remains in a white Chinese food carton.

It had reeked. Still did, but the spices are intoxicating. He can smell them now.

Burning, uneaten kimchee, soaked into Hitler's shirt. Hiram's stomach growls again.

Hitler had turned up his mustachioed nose to the stuff. "What is it?" He'd eyed the food suspiciously. "It smells rotten," he'd frowned.

"Just eat it," barked Hiram. "It's fermented cabbage. You should like it…"

"It's like sauerkraut," Hiram had offered.

"It smells awful."

"Then hold your fucking nose."

Hitler had refused.

In a rage of alcoholic fury, at gunpoint, Hiram had ended up forcing the rotten cabbage into Hitler's mouth, smearing it onto his shirt, mussing it into his hair.

Another wave of mushroom dementia washes over him. The shrooms and the opium aren't getting along. Aren't playing nice. They're doing naughty, crazy things together. Hiram feels the room stretching out in all directions around him, the wooden floorboards bowing and rippling and sliding in strange tidal waves. His eyeballs are trying to roll out of his head. He clenches his eyelids shut, intent on keeping them in—then worries that they might roll too deep inside—might get lost in the gray tangle of his brains. Hiram can't imagine a worse eternity than being trapped and staring at the dark inner workings of his mind, an unblinking voyeur lost in the maze of his own demons…

It's the asceticism of the binge. No food. It's the hunger talking—the dirty, unwashed smelliness of his sweat-soaked, unchanged clothes. No sleep, no eat… the wide-eyed horror… The strange, tidal *necessity* of it all

The opium and mushrooms are taking over now. Growing roots and taking deep control of his under-mind. Hiram can feel the *Glenfiddich* saturating his veins. Seeping into his brainstem, the cradle of life. Feeding those groping, growing roots of psychedelic dementia… Taking hold… He is losing himself. Losing control. Losing his mind, and…

And…

There's only one thing to do. Only one thing to be done. Only one solution…

Absinthe.

The answer would be found at the bottom of a bottle of absinthe. The Girls would know what to do, *Mother*, *Sadie*, and the *Green fairy*…

The Girls…

Twelve Little Hitlers… One down and eleven to go…

Oh, and Jodie… always, there is Jodie…

To be continued in
Hiram Grange & the Twelve Little Hitlers…

A passionate novelist and short fiction writer, **Scott Christian Carr** makes a living as a writer and producer currently working in film and television. He is the Sr. Writer/Co-Creator of The Learning Channel (TLC) series *Dead Tenants*. His company, Brothers Carr Productions, was recently awarded 1st Place in Scriptapalooza TV for Best Original Pilot for their show *The REAL Deal*.

Scott is the creator and executive producer of the scifi film *The NUKE Brothers* and writer of the tie-in comic book *The Continuing Adventures of Fat Man and Little Boy*. He's currently shoulder deep in the production of his feature film *The Men In the Moon* as well as the upcoming television series *The Mole People*.

Scott's fiction has appeared in dozens of magazines and publications, and he was awarded The Hunter S. Thompson Award for Outstanding Journalism in 1999 for his para-sociological news journal *The Flying Saucer Gazette*. His books, *Desolate Places*, *Beneath the Surface* and *Sick: An Anthology of Illness*, are available at Amazon or your local bookseller.

Visit Scott at *www.myspace.com/sardy*.

An Interview with Ronald Damien Malfi
by Tim Lieder

Since his first novel, the gothic horror The Fall of Never, *Ronald Damien Malfi has built a reputation as a solid horror writer with an eye for detail and a mastery of language. His latest work,* Passenger, *is a noir-tinged psychological mystery about a man who wakes up on a bus without memory.*
With allusions to The Odyssey *and a walking tour through the ugly streets of Baltimore,* Passenger *is quickly becoming Ronald's most popular work..*

TIM: How would you describe *Passenger*?

RDM: I consider it a dark humanist drama with satirical overtones. At times horrific. When Delirium picked it up I was concerned, since Delirium has a horror market reputation and I didn't consider it a straight horror novel.

I don't find vampires or zombies particularly scary. I find fear in real people, situations, nuance and color. I'm also trying to honestly serve the story without playing into the trappings of the genre. I'm not going to throw a car crash into chapter 3 because it needs a car crash. Some appreciate it. Others would prefer vampires.

TIM: Your character refers to a lava filled world several times. Where does that come from?

RDM: That phrase I made up but it's a variation on the language of the different Baltimore residents that I would run into at my favorite bars. Throughout college, my friends and I would go to these places, sit and drink and just listen to the colorful characters that came in. All the bars in the place are based on real places. I very much wanted to make Baltimore into a character. This is the second in what I consider my Baltimore trilogy.

TIM: The first was *The Nature of Monsters*.

RDM: Yes, that was satirical and overly colorful. This one is more of a snapshot of the city from a very bleak and introverted perspective.

TIM: Have you seen *The Wire*?

RDM: Yes, it was filmed near where I work. I wouldn't say that I was directly influenced by *The Wire*. They are doing their own thing and I'm doing mine.

TIM: This book is very reminiscent of film noir. Was there any film noir classic that influenced you?

RDM: Not directly. I enjoy the Coen Brothers' work. There's a book out by Ethan Coen, *Gates of Eden*, which is a short story collection based on their movies. I enjoyed that immensely.

Author Spotlight
Ronald Damien Malfi

For this book in particular, I had to go to my bookshelf and reread my collection. One particular work, *Bud Wing* by Evan Hunter, worried me. It begins like *Passenger* with a guy waking up on a park bench without his memory. One of things I ask myself when I write a book is, "Has this been done?" because I don't want to rewrite someone else's work. The reasons behind the memory loss are not the same and my book goes in a different direction. I can also sit down and watch *Maltese Falcon* any time, but it's not a direct influence.

TIM: Was there a direct influence?

RDM: When I first started writing it, I wanted a modern version of *The Odyssey*. You still see the allusions to it, from the one eyed fortune teller in the Chinese restaurant to the three sirens represented as strippers.

TIM: Why *The Odyssey*?

RDM: Homer's *The Odyssey* is the ultimate literal journey. The protagonist in Passenger is on his own journey, though more of a spiritual, moral and internalized one. The parallels were too great to ignore, although I diluted the direct allusions to Homer's work between the final book and the initial draft. A solitary man's struggle to return to who he is and where he comes from—be it literal or figurative, outward or internal—has always fascinated me.

TIM: Since the main character has no memory, he begins to make up his identity. Was that a conscious decision on your part to let him build his own identity?

RDM: He is just making up his identity as a way of doing something. I didn't plan that out. If I know how a novel is going to end, I won't write it. I just begin with a rough sketch. In this case I wanted to present Baltimore as a character to a man who is both alien to the city and to himself.

TIM: What made you want to write about Baltimore?

RDM: The city is continuously in a state of metamorphosis; its topography constantly in flux. Like lava rushing through the streets, the city is in constant transition.

RDM: I used to sing and play guitar in a band for a few years. We'd play in these places around Baltimore. Some bars had stages. Others had hovels in the basement. One place was across the street from a strip club and the strippers would come in and listen after our sets. It is still one of the most colorful places I've worked.

TIM: What did your band play?

RDM: It was the mid-90s and we started out as a cover band. Lot of alternative. When I worked on original material it was like a combination between Tool and Live. Poppy but a little off. When I played piano, I played everything from background music to jazz and boogie-woogie. That's why almost all of my novels make the music into a primary character.

TIM: You've used jazz as a metaphor in the past. How is it different in this book?

RDM: In *Via Dolorosa* jazz is used as a symbolic temptation of infidelity that faced Nick, the main character. Even the musician in *Via Dolorosa*, Russell "Goatman" Claxton, was a human embodiment of the devil himself—from the "goat man" moniker to the name of his most popular jazz record, "Mephistopheles"—and he was bent on driving Nick farther and farther down the path of temptation. In *Passenger* the jazz music serves to underscore the grittiness of the city itself. In fact, they don't just play jazz, the protagonist plays raucous barrelhouse barroom boogie-woogie, steeped in grimy, animalistic undertones, which is one of the notes I wanted to carry throughout the novel.

TIM: You based many of the locations on real places. What are some of the real places like?

RDM: Cat's Eye Pub is the basis for The Neighborhood. It's actually in Fell's Point, the college part of the city and it's much less depressing than the other places where the novel takes place. Outside are old cobblestone paths and water nearby. It's so insulated that it doesn't even have its own Web site, but myspace is littered with mentions.

Other places in the novel are the neighborhoods with the warehouses and the highways overhead. Very grim places. I played piano in a Chinese restaurant similar to the one in the novel. Other Baltimore scenes like the Old Bay snorting contest, I made up but based on fact.

TIM: What's Old Bay?

RDM: Old Bay is a spicy seasoning that they put on Maryland crabs. It crystallizes on the powder and has a very paprika taste. It's very much a Baltimore spice, unique to the area. You always hear about people drinking it in shots or eating it whole so a snorting contest isn't off base.

TIM: Was Clarence based on a real character?

RDM: Clarence isn't based on anyone in particu-

lar, but I wanted him to embody the city as a literary tour guide. He's a comedic satire of a typical Baltimore resident but he's also a plot thread that pops up whenever the story seems to be moving slowly.

Clarence is Baltimore—the confusion, the distaste, the evolution, the dejected, the downtrodden… but he is the hopeful, the loving, the understanding, the soldier. He's a bad guy who does good and a good guy who is bad. A conundrum, which is how I see the city of Baltimore. The city's motto is "Believe," touted from banners and billboards, yet the streets are overrun with homelessness and disease. That's Clarence, too—do you trust him or distrust him? Is he a hero or a thug? I'll leave that open to the audience, although I believe that he is a hero.

Excerpt from... Hiram Grange & the Digital Eucharist
Robert Davies

The five corpses formed a meticulous circle of outstretched limbs and broken necks. Each chest had been splayed open, the skin lovingly peeled back and the ribcage cracked and split apart. Several organs had been plucked out and placed at various points along the glimmering circumference of the warding circle. Glistening lengths of blue-black intestine snaked around each corpse, twining with the arms and legs of the next body. At each of the four compass points, 7-11 Big Gulp cups held a frothy syrup of blood, hot red pepper flakes, and semen. Nineteen flickering Yankee Candles filled the abandoned subway station with the reek of lilacs, frankincense, and burning citrus.

At the center of this summoning circle, naked and sheathed in sweat, buzzing with Red Bull and Adderall, stood Roger Millis, 48 years old, balding, henpecked husband, father of five, self-proclaimed adept of the Art, stumbling over the many-layered incantation he had struggled for weeks to memorize.

Millis was coming to the last quatrain when he saw a man walking along the abandoned train tracks, whistling and twirling an ebony cane. His immaculate white linen suit and hat shone in the darkness. Millis watched as the stranger leapt from the tracks onto the platform and sauntered toward the warding circle, clicking his cane on the concrete with every step.

The stranger took in the scene with aplomb, walking around the circle, shaking his head. "This is sloppy work, Mr. Millis. Sloppy work indeed."

Millis felt his insides freeze. He could not move.

The man in white pointed with his cane.

"Look, the positions of the organs are all wrong. Cooling lungs have a stronger influence on the pneuma when placed on the left. And here, look! Kidneys should never, ever face the south. Children know that." The stranger paused beside one of the corpses. "This looks like the work of an epileptic butcher. Christ! These incisions are brutal. Where's your sense of art? Where's your pride, man?"

The stranger knelt down and grabbed a prostitute's head by the hair and turned it to see her face. "Ah, she does look like Ms. Foster, doesn't she? At least you did that right. They all could pass for Hiram's beloved Jodie in the right lighting. I pray he can see this before their flesh wilts. Oh, what joy it would have been to have had the real Jodie Foster for the summoning, eh? I think young master Grange would positively shatter then. Alas, these strumpets will have to do."

The stranger then knelt at the edge of the summoning circle. "But this here is simply unforgivable. These summoning words. These letters are barely decipherable."

Millis found the last remnant of his spine. "What do you know of the Golden Helico Text?" He had emptied out his 401K, his daughters' college funds, and sold all his rare coins and Civil War memorabilia on eBay to get enough money for it.

"Well, for starters, old boy, I own the original copy," the stranger said.

Millis was shocked to silence.

"It proved invaluable when I made the forgery that you came across. That I, ah, allowed you to find."

Millis' mouth went dry.

"Oh, yes, it was a masterwork, if I can be so crass as to congratulate myself. I chewed the insects myself to get that ink color correct, and I flayed three crippled lambs for their skins. An exact copy, down to that damn carved bone frontispiece." The stranger grinned widely. "Of course, I took some liberties, tweaking the text a little, shuffling a few names around, tainting a few spells."

Millis felt the ice inside him reach his testicles. "What have you done to me?"

"To you? Not a thing. You are merely cheese in the trap. An ambitious little snack who is going to summon the biggest fucking mouse this city has seen in ages. What *it* does to you? Well, I trust that will not be pleasant at all."

Millis could not control his shaking now. He could barely breathe. "I just wanted a succubus."

The stranger in white laughed again. "So you have scrawled here. In your blood and seed no less. Truly pathetic. One does not summon demons of the Abyss using the letters of the Alphabet. Those empty things pass the mouths of morons, lovers, and priests every single day. No, you need something rather different. Look! These are what you need, here, there, and those sigils there." The man in white pointed out the dark, writhing runes that rose from the marked circle, glowing and throbbing, refusing any one shape. "Those are the bleeding letters of the Omegabet. I seeded your little cantrip with them. Put a bit of a different worm on your hook, as it were. Face it, old boy; you're summoning a fish for the ages."

Millis' eyes ached as the glowing letters throbbed. The hearts of the five corpses began to pulse in time, and pale hands slowly dragged themselves across the sand until they found cold vaginas and cruel knife cuts. With a frantic intensity the dead worried at themselves, fingering their wounds, greedily sucking in air through their damp, slit throats. Globules of their revitalized blood began to float, spiraling around the circle.

> "And inside him, inside his massive, boiling womb, a fanged, rough thing writhed with abandon, frantic for release."

Millis at last could read the name of the demon burning among the letters. "Giblis," he whispered. Hot piss ran down his legs.

"Got it on the first try! The very one," the stranger said. "He's one of the Unmakers, I do believe. A bit out of your league, little adept. Nevertheless, he is on his way, and I trust he will be a tad ravenous."

"What is that you want from me? Please."

"Oh, don't be silly. This is not a bartering session. You are a dead man. That is quite out of my hands." The man in white smiled. He removed a small pouch from an inside pocket. He pulled out a bullet and laid it on the edge of the circle. He took a few steps, took out a bottle of absinthe and splashed the stones. The last thing he pulled from the pouch was a tattered scrap of cloth. He sniffed it and grimaced. "Your taste in cologne was always so gauche, Hiram Grange." He dropped the cloth inside the circle and turned to go.

"Wait! Where are you going? What is this?"

The man turned, grinning. "Those are merely, ah, offerings for the demon when he is born. To remind him who his friends are. And his enemies. Nothing you need concern yourself with."

"B- b- born?"

The man in white smiled. "You did not read the text to the very end, did you?" He laughed one last time. "Just remember. Deep breaths, old boy. Deep breaths."

His mother had died in childbirth, and it was now clear that Roger Millis was going to do the same. The pain made him detached from the atrocity that his flesh had become, swollen, pustulent, taut, brimming with the aching energy of the Abyss seeking to enter this later world, the world beneath, the world of blood and bone. Five pair of eyes watched his excruciating transformation, the five nameless whores whom he had plied with drugs and twenties, filled with fast food and hot seed, and then slit their pale throats, five offerings in a foolish gambit that he never truly understood. Millis had spent the last three months prowling the downtown streets of several nearby cities and towns, and he posted many ads online and lingered in strange chat rooms, all the while looking for Jodie Foster lookalikes. He never once stopped to question the text. It was in black and white, it had to be true. When he found the five he needed, he brought them all, one at a time, to a motel on Rt.128. He gave them heroin, pills, and vodka and let them play their heavy metal ballads or their hardcore gangsta rap as they danced in the glaring headlights of passing cars. He would climb on top of them and give it the old college try. After he wiped himself off, he broke their necks.

He saved the cutting for the subway station.

The five Jodies drooled black fluid now, carelessly stumbling over their spilled innards, a syrupy, ropy mess that muddied their slow, circular progression around him. They spoke, but not any words he understood. Harsh syllables marred by thick, clotting blood and rotting throats filled the air. Their dissolution was beautiful in its own way, if a tad rancid, and they clearly still had some siren allure from their sidewalk days, for throughout the long, aching, sunless hours, Millis watched as homeless men and runaway teenagers and businessmen in fancy suits and stomachs filled with olives and martinis snuck into the station, called on by their loins, and he watched as the horny men disrobed and silently embraced the rotting hookers and allowed themselves to be torn open by broken glass bottles and jagged fingernails. He could never turn away, and when it was over, the irrational hunger would rise inside him until it burned. The Jodies would bring pieces to his growing form. No matter how much he tried to fight it, in the end Millis would end up feasting on the hot muscle, the lungs and the heart, and the congealing liquor of their dying life.

And inside him, inside his massive, boiling womb, a fanged, rough thing writhed with abandon, frantic for release. His swollen abdomen, pale and immense, beggared reason, nestled as it was in a pile of entrails and offal that shivered with maggots and a million glimmers off the buzzing wings of flies.

The five throatless prostitutes provided their own mad language, competing with the drone with their own insensate chanting.

At long last, Millis felt his skin split. The burning pain was secondary to the relief that it would soon be over. A hooked talon poked through, grasping the edge of skin and pulling, stretching both the skein of reality and the sweat-sheened skin of his stomach. It tore at both with vigor and bleeding glee, eager to be born into the world, pulling itself from the gelid, congealed amnion of the eternal Abyss into the warm fetor of the subway station. Millis' ribs cracked and bones shattered as the demon burst from the wound in his womb, but miraculously Hollis lived, his life hanging upon the jagged thorn of the demon's puissance. He was both witness and midwife, the explosive ruin of his lower torso left him mute, a macabre mermaid that was part man, part bloody ruination.

Millis could only stare in awe as the blood-shiny demon stretched to its full height, spraying vast torrents of meconium into the shadows as it flexed its newly incarnated muscles. The air grew hot.

He had been such a fool. This was no simple demon or flibbertigibbet to be hex-driven into mortal service, no dim-witted succubus to be coaxed to orgasm with gold or rare gem. This was Giblis, one of the Unmakers, birthed in the darkness before the stars, servant of the eternal Abyss. A breathing marriage of scaled flesh and raging flame, the demon glowed from within with a bloody incandescence. Its skin was a thin veil over the boiling malevolence that seethed just underneath, and here and there rips and tears in its flesh allowed a virulent flame to burn through. A small serpentine corpse-rider coiled around the demon's massive right arm; three of its brethren swarmed on the demon's back and shoulders. The corpse-riders chattered maniacally when they were not gorging themselves on thick flakes of the demon's smoldering skin.

Millis felt his life slipping away, and he was glad for it. Before his eyes, the demon Giblis sniffed the air, as though sensing something painful. Millis felt the strange bond with his offspring, could almost know its ancient thoughts. The demon's preternatural senses filled Millis with confusion. The cloying scent of burnt poppies. Absinthe. The moist stink of desperation, patchouli, sweaty sex. The tell-tale attar of an adept, a hunter.

The Unmaker seemed to recognize the smell, and his face split with a vicious grin.

Giblis whirled, his massive arm shattering the spine of one of the midwives, one of the luckless Jodies. The demon roared, shaking the tracks. "Grange!"

He screamed again and then shook off the four serpentine corpse riders.

"Find him!" The lithe creatures darted away, chattering in their mad, aboriginal tongue. "Find Hiram Grange!"

The four dead prostitutes left standing screamed with malodorous joy. Millis' last sight was to see the prostitutes as one rush forward to lick and caress the demon's still smoldering skin.

There were too many coincidences, too many truths that he had failed to see. That he had not allowed himself to see. This was something more than a wet job against a charismatic leader. This was a trap. The levers and the gears were artfully concealed,

> "The demon's preternatural senses filled Millis with confusion. The cloying scent of burnt poppies. Absinthe. The moist stink of desperation, patchouli, sweaty sex."

but they moved with a certainty that Hiram could no longer ignore. He had to go underground. He had to see for himself that the demon Giblis was still bound, as he had left it years ago.

Because if it was not, then everything would change.

The area had undergone some major renovations in the decades since he had first come here. Abandoned factories and worn-down tenements given way to expensive condominiums and posh restaurants. The Combat Zone, with its neon-blinking sex shops, smoke-filled peep shows, and $10 whores with needle-bit arms had been swept away and replaced by theaters and posh venues, merely whores of another stripe. Grange wasn't sure the change was all that different. It was merely a bandage over a festering wound, and the quality of the band-aid could do little to stem the slow, certain rise of pus and stinking odor of sickness that rose from the cold, sterile streets.

He descended the escalator at the Downtown Crossing station and passed into the station proper. A service entrance allowed him into a utility hallway that ran parallel to the outbound tracks. Several flights of stairs brought him deeper into the earth. At last, his way was blocked by a room stuffed with old machine parts and thick, useless pipes, and rusted filing cabinets filled with musty, mildewed papers from the mid-70s. The green smell of mold filled his senses. But he pressed on, forcing himself through a narrow vent, and down a thin, rickety air duct that sliced his skin as he passed. The rumble of passing trains and the screeching of their metal wheels made his teeth ache, and the pop and hiss of the electrified third rail illuminated the thin slits in the air duct. After several minutes, Hiram dropped from a rust-worn vent into a small, darkened room. Broken glass crunched underfoot and the walls were shiny with dripping, oily water. The door handle came off in his hand and he made his way onto the abandoned West platform of the Grey Line.

The smells that assailed him answered his question immediately. Burned, rotting meat, the acrid scent of smoldering hair, congealed blood, the ashen scent of the Abyss. Across the platform, Grange could see the teeming pile of white, roiling maggots and the lashing tails of soot-darkened rats. He hopped onto the tracks and made his way across to the other platform, carefully avoiding the third rail, though it should have been inert for decades. He could leave nothing to chance now. His hand reached for his holster and found the heavy comfort of his Webley. He had filled the five chambers with demon shot, bullets throated with mercury and white gold dust.

The reptilian stench told him he had been wise to do so.

Hiram pulled himself up onto the platform and warily approached the birthing pile. He cracked open a flare from his satchel. Its red glow illuminated the underground chamber. He tossed it into the pile of carrion eaters. The rats scurried away, but the maggots sizzled in their idiot greed. In the shifting red light, Grange could see the fragments of human body parts and the splinters of broken bone. A pile of livers and hearts was set off to the side, but there were far too many pieces to have any concept of how many had died here to give Giblis his freedom. Fragments of a warding circle were hidden now beneath the spreading slime of corruption, the eldritch energies long faded from the sigils and precise lines.

Hiram felt something inside come undone. Knowing that the demon was free released a fierce tension that Grange had not known was there. An empty malaise was now filled with the certainty of what he would be facing. It steeled him, gave him a solid purpose. It made his trigger finger itch. This time he wouldn't banish the demon back to the Abyss. No, he would rip it apart, dance on its insides, and shit on the sticky mess. He was going to destroy the very memory of the fucking scaly beast.

Grange tensed and felt the hairs on his neck rise. He felt exposed. Something predatory watched from the shadows. Grange planted his feet and slowly eased the Webley from his holster, cocking the hammer back.

A broken thing burst from the shadows, a shattered corpse with the angelic face of Jodie Foster. She pulled herself across the cement with ruined hands, trailing lengths of dusty intestine behind her. The bone of her shattered spine scraped on the cement. She grasped onto Grange's legs with frozen hands and started to pull herself up, a puppy happy to see its master, only this beast was delirious with insatiable hunger, clawing and snapping at him with shattered teeth. The hot, sour stench of death punched into him, stinging his eyes and making him gag. Grange kicked her away and pulled up the Webley, and he fired a shot directly into her skull. She slammed on the platform with a wet slap.

The explosion echoed in the abandoned subway, and his ears rang with the violence of it. The pleasing scent of cordite hid the charnel scent for a moment, and Grange sucked it in greedily.

He needed his pipe. He needed a drink. He needed someone warm. Gnashing teeth and clawing would be fine, as long as she was warm.

To be continued in
Hiram Grange & the Digital Eucharist....

Rob Davies writes stories about voracious babies, exploding suns, stuff that hasn't happened yet, and crippled angels. He lives in Somerville, Massachusetts, with his wife Sara, their two cats, Lilith and Tiamat, a lot of books, millions of oxygen atoms, a few plants, and a sometimes tickle in his throat.

Rob's story "Angel, Rape, Wheelchair" appeared in *Shroud* #3, and his writings have stained the pages of the likes of *Interzone* and *Arkham Tales*. He is currently at work on his novel, *The Matter of Upright Beasts*.

More news from Rob can be found on his website, *Dumb Angel*, at *www.robertedavies.com*.

WALK LIKE THE DEAD
STORY & PHOTOS BY CONOR POWERS-SMITH

The kid might've expected trouble, coming into the City in his Cape Cod hoodie and Red Sox cap. To say nothing of the company he's been keeping. All day long he's walked the streets of the Lower East Side of Manhattan with what looks like several hundred shuffling corpses. He's listened to their grunts and groans of cannibal hunger, and he's smiled.

All day long the things have left him alone; maybe there were too many other potential sources of nourishment, among the Sunday throngs on the streets and sidewalks, for them to notice the one small meal in their midst. But now, as they wander into Washington Square Park, nearly deserted as dusk falls, as the sun sinks and the shadows stretch across the ground, there's nothing to distract them, and they begin to take notice.

A hand falls heavily on the kid's right shoulder, and there's a low, throaty groan—different from the mindless, generalized sounds he's been hearing all day: more articulate, somehow; more specific. Before he can even turn, there's a hand on his other shoulder, then one on his left arm, then two there, then three, the stiff, clumsy fingers digging into his sleeve, and, beneath that, into his skin, and beneath that, into the meat of his arm. More groans go up from all directions, and the knot of vaguely human forms surrounding him collapses in.

Cold gray skin obscures the kid, as if the shadows themselves are attacking. Very quickly he's dragged to the ground, his arms and legs held spread-eagle. His unzipped sweatshirt is brushed aside, and the plain white T-shirt beneath is shredded. Hands move with greedy impatience to his exposed belly. Heads descend, mouths gaping, teeth poised. Mercifully, the last, inevitable act is hidden by the bobbing heads and hunched, hyena-like shoulders. The kid screams, once.

Eventually, as if by some unspoken signal, the things raise their heads and draw back. They struggle to their feet, and shamble off into the shadows. The kid lies still for perhaps a minute. Then he rises. His movements are stiff. His balance, when he finally gains his feet, appears precarious. His eyes stare vacantly ahead. He groans, tentatively, as if unsure. Answering groans sound from the shadows all around him.

He shuffles slowly, aimlessly away, the tatters of his T-shirt flapping loosely around his red-smeared chest and stomach. For a few minutes he's discernible, among the shadowy forms that fill the park, by his Red Sox cap,

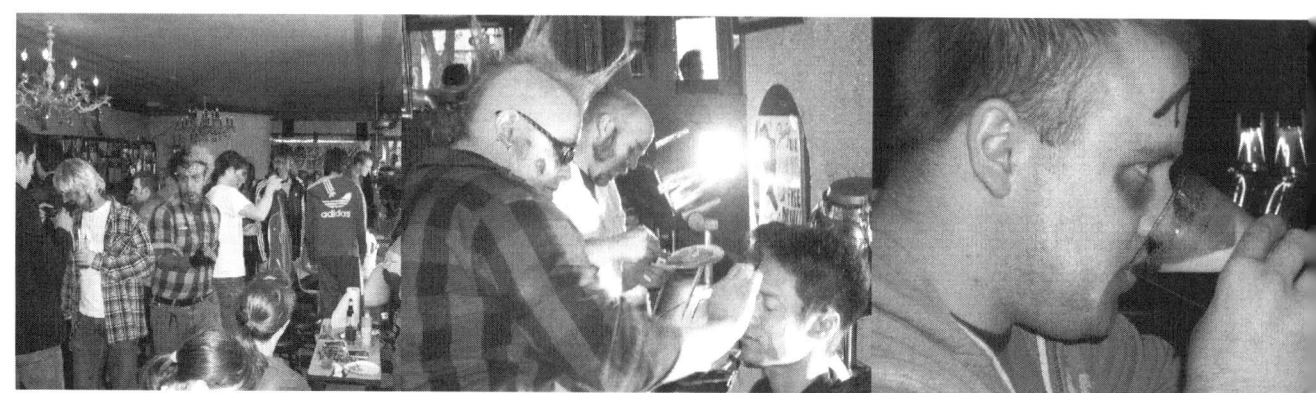

Shroud 5   The Journal of Dark Fiction and Art

ZOMBIE HORROR STUNS MANHATTAN

which has somehow remained in place. Then even that fades into the gloom, and the only indication that the kid was ever here is the wet red stain, glinting dully in the last vanishing shreds of daylight, on the cold stone ground where, briefly, he lay.

Sunday the 26th of October was World Zombie Day, and in New York, as in nearly 50 other cities around the world, the date was observed in the only manner appropriate: a zombie walk. Something like three hundred fifty people came together, dressed and made-up to resemble the recently deceased. They walked the streets of the Lower East Side in a moaning, shambling pack, snapping and snarling at passersby, attacking cars and buses, frightening the easily frightened.

Don't ask why. If the idea of shuffling around all day in torn clothes and about five pounds of makeup, stage blood and prosthetic wounds doesn't appeal to you immediately, it probably never will. This isn't something you could learn, even if you wanted to. You have to be, so to speak, bitten by it.

And, as the bitten will tell you, the hunger, once incited, will never disappear. There is no known vaccine, and the only possible treatment is the deed itself. Once a year, or twice, or as many times as they can manage, the devotees of the dead will rise, and clothe themselves in the cerements of the crypt—or jeans and a T-shirt, or a pair of pajamas; you know, depending—and take to the streets, arms extended in desperate hunger, eyes rolled back and glassy, feet just barely maintaining equilibrium as they shuffle along in their slow, palsied stride.

They will walk in Paris. They will walk in London, England and London, Canada. They will walk in Sydney, and Copenhagen, and San Francisco. They will walk, in their largest numbers, in the birthplace of the modern zombie mythos, Pittsburgh, Pennsylvania. And they will walk in the capital of the world.

Properly speaking, the New York event is a zombie pub crawl, or zombie crawl, a subcategory of zombie walk in which at least two stops on the route are bars. The rallying point in this case is the Beauty Bar, a strange combination night club/beauty parlor on East Fourteenth Street. A well-stocked bar occupies one side of the narrow, black-and-white-tiled space; 50s-style salon chairs with big chrome overhead hairdryers line the opposite wall.

Most walkers arrive already in

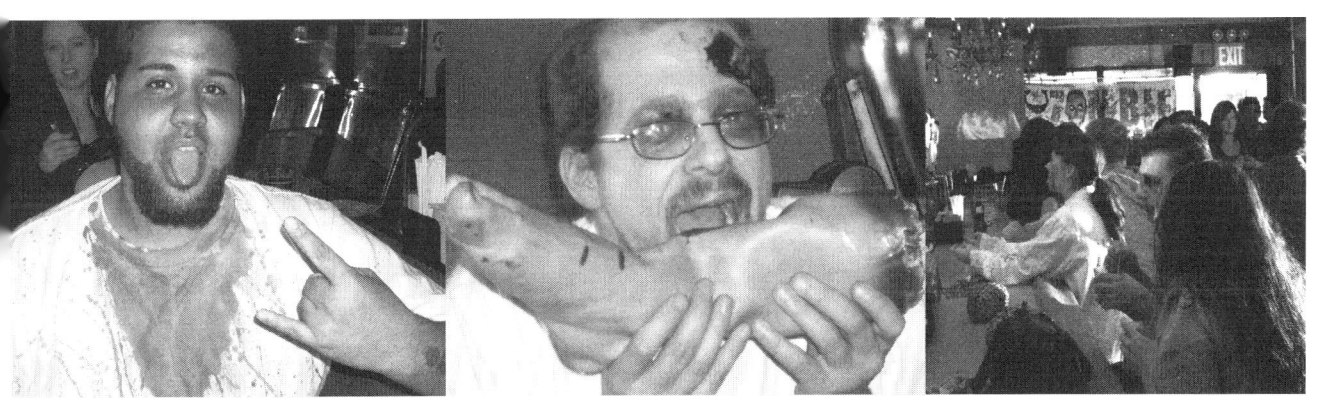

full makeup, but for those who need it, friendly zombie makeup artists are on hand to help. From two to four in the afternoon, there's a constant influx of aspiring zombies in need of attention, and the salon side of the place is at least as busy as the bar side. Mirrors and makeup kits and small, super-bright photography lights cover every available surface. The walkers sink back into the vinyl and receive layer after layer of green and blue and black and red. Blow dryers speed the process. One makeup zombie, her body a shapely mass of sickly green and lurid red, displays a quantity of cleavage apparently intended to make one reevaluate his attitudes toward necrophilia.

Across the room at the bar, zombies sip whiskey and beer, and check each other out. Many of them have put some serious time, effort and cash into their costumes. The best easily beat out ninety percent of modern movie effects. Even the simplest would fit seamlessly into Romero's original masterpiece, *Night of the Living Dead*, which was made in 1968 for about a buck-fifty.

If the costumes inspire competition, it's confined to the quiet hours of planning and preparation before the event. Here in the Beauty Bar, comments are universally appreciative and complimentary. Many zombies are proud of their costumes, and rightly so. But it doesn't dampen their enjoyment of other people's approaches.

By two-thirty or three the place is effectively full. Zombies keep shuffling in, and a party atmosphere rises very naturally to the surface. Before long a solid, steady chatter rises from the mingling ghouls, and laughter forms a significant part of it. Whatever self-consciousness might inevitably come with being seen in public covered with makeup and splattered with stage blood—maybe with an eyeball dangling from one socket, or the eraser-end of a pencil projecting from a realistic-looking puncture wound—is gone now, washed away in the tide of mutual enthusiasm and booze.

Out on the sidewalk in front of the bar a similar scene is building, with the added element of a curious audience. Dozens of zombies—smokers, under-twenty-ones, non-drinkers, attention-seekers—are stacking up out here almost by the minute. And passersby are taking notice, many stopping for a few minutes to talk and take pictures with the grisly—though strangely genial—undead. Some just stand and gawk. Of course, some look

Shroud 5   The Journal of Dark Fiction and Art

away and pretend, in that unconvincing but persistent New York way, to be completely unaffected by the spectacle.

Some even hurry their pace as they cut a path through the milling dead. A woman with a stroller rushes through the crowd, darting nervous glances back and forth as if this pack of weirdoes and maniacs might unleash some unimaginable form of madness on her and her baby at any moment. But the baby, maybe six or eight months old, clearly having failed to associate these people with anything it might consider scary or wrong, is smiling up at them serenely.

Some couples are here together, and many have settled on a theme to set themselves apart from the rest. There's the Mexican bandito zombie, with his wide sombrero and blood-stained serape, with his thick, drooping black mustache and bandolier stocked with shot glasses; naturally he's accompanied by a deceased senorita, whose short barmaid skirt and lacy, low-cut blouse once again throw society's traditional disapproval of necrophilia into serious question. There's a nurse and her patient, both far beyond the reach of medical science; multiple matching prom couples, multiple pairs of newlyweds. There's Alice and the White Rabbit: beneath his bunny hood, with its floppy ears and bright white fur, the rabbit's mouth and chin and chest are caked with blood, obviously corresponding to a gaping bite wound in Alice's throat.

Among the vastly outnumbered living participants is a couple with matching blood-splattered goggles and oversized plastic machetes. On the front of their yellow shirts is printed ZOM-BE-GONE: HUNTERS FOR HIRE; on the back, THE ONLY GOOD ZOMBIE IS A DEAD ZOMBIE. If they work on commission, this should be a big day for them; assuming they survive.

Some of the most memorable costumes hint at some kind of back-story, or at least invite speculation as to what the zombie was in life, or what he or she was doing at the time of death. A Hawaiian shirt, lei and beachball suffice, or a bathrobe and hair curlers. Truckers, tourists, boy scouts and pizza chefs are represented. Maybe the most mutely eloquent zombie is the girl in the red jogging shorts, with a marathon-runner's number pinned to her shirt, and leaves, no doubt from the scene of her gruesome death, still clinging to her hair.

Shortly past four, Doug Sakmann, the event's organizer—decked out in the red-and-white-striped jacket of a carnival barker, his skin a pale, lifeless blue—leads the zombies still inside the Beauty Bar out into the daylight, and the walk begins. Spread three or four abreast on the sidewalk, the horde extends for a city block or more. The brutish moans and cries of "brains" are loud and constant, the palsied gaits fine and varied.

The weather's pretty much ideal. Yesterday and all last night the whole tri-state area was thrashed by strong wind and heavy rain, but today dawned clear and bright, and the horde has blue skies to shamble under, and temperatures in the high fifties and low sixties to warm its cold collective blood.

Photographers follow the horde down East Fourteenth Street,

snapping away on cheap disposable cameras or expensive digital SLRs. Some drop off and go about their business after a block or so, others stick with the crawl pretty much until the end. In the next four or five hours there will be no point at which at least a dozen photographers aren't moving around at the periphery of the horde, like those little parasitic fish that swim along behind sharks.

Two blocks west on East Fourteenth takes the walkers to Union Square. At the park's southeast corner the horde breaks up and flows down three or four separate paths, like a river temporarily splitting off into tributaries. One path turns out to lead directly past a Christian rock band in mid-performance. Some zombies ignore the sudden, not-universally-favorable attention this draws from the band's fans; a few, their depraved instincts momentarily soothed by the bubbly melodies, take to the stage. The band deals with this remarkably well: the music never slows, and the big, Good-News grins never falter.

The streams flow together again for a group picture at the base of the Independence Flagstaff. The walkers pile in close, some climbing up to stand or crouch or lie flat on top of the high, wide pedestal. The gathered horde goes through countless rounds of coordinated screaming and face-making and menacing-gesturing. After ten or fifteen minutes the zombies start to get a little restless, but there's always one more photo to be taken. It's basically your high school class picture, if your school had hired Tom Savini to take it, and then paid him exclusively in bad acid.

When the photo session's over, the horde moves out of the park and across the street to the Whole Foods supermarket. Each walker needs to obtain at least one nonperishable food item, which will be donated to a world hunger charity. Yes, seriously. But it makes sense: it's in a zombie's best interest to keep as many people alive and well-fed as possible, in the same sense that it's in a Kobe cattle rancher's best interests to fatten up his stock on beer and regular sake-massages. Because, eventually....

Whole Foods has been informed of the descending zombie plague: store employees regard the walkers pouring through the doors with some interest, but no surprise. But nobody's bothered to tell the customers about it. Judging by their faces, the invasion is distressingly unexpected.

Bystander reactions are different inside than out. On the street, reactions are generally positive: smiles, compliments, the occasional cathartic, laughter-tinged shriek of mock terror. People seem to accept this for what it is, whatever that might be. Outside there's the implicit, ever-present awareness of open space and potential running room.

Inside, you're always cornered. Even if your conscious mind isn't aware of it, some primitive, survival-motivated part of you certainly is. Three hundred rotting corpses suddenly bearing down on you from all directions—and God help your shattered mind if you happen to be in the canned food aisle of that particular supermarket at that particular moment—isn't something you can

bypass or ignore, if there's nowhere else to go, and if your whole field of vision is full of the loathsome things.

Which is not to suggest that these unsuspecting shoppers believe they're literally in danger of being torn apart and devoured, probably while still technically alive. Many of them don't appear to know what a zombie is, let alone its preferred diet or mode of behavior. But the instinctive leeriness of the unusual is operating much more strongly in Whole Foods than anywhere else on the route.

The express checkout line now resembles the line for an amusement park ride on a busy day, snaking around corners, blocking whole rows of shelves, effectively shutting down the salad bar. A stock boy, holding a big red sign reading END, has been dispatched to stand behind the last person in line, in an attempt to avoid confusion. The zombies wait patiently to pay, and trickle out of the store in ones and twos, to join the tight knot of corpses on the sidewalk outside. The crowd is so thick out here that pedestrians are obliged to either shoulder through the horde or take their chances in the street.

The last can of organic tuna finally paid for, the walk recommences, the horde briefly heading east again before turning south onto Broadway. Traffic is sparse, and someone calls out, "Fill the street!" The call is picked up on

all sides, and the walkers do as bidden, spreading out to both sides, seizing the entire street as their own. This may be the walk's single most striking image: the implacable army of the risen dead, hundreds strong, pressed together shoulder-to-shoulder, lurching unchallenged down the center of the street.

The next stop is Halloween Adventure, a block-deep costume shop on Broadway and East Eleventh. The walkers are instructed to file through, drop off their foodstuffs, and exit out the other side, which gives onto Fourth Ave. The crowd bottlenecks at the door; about half get through before traffic has to be stopped to let a long line of waiting customers out.

The place was packed before the zombies ever arrived. Some of the customers are amused by the horde—one Latino man says jovially to his young child, "Mira los locos"— but generally the reaction is subdued, lacking even the animal wariness so evident in Whole Foods. These people are like mall shoppers on the last weekend before Christmas; they've been neck-deep in the commercial end of Halloween for hours, and they've simply ODed.

On the other side of the store, out on Fourth Ave., the zombies have taken to accosting cars and buses to pass the time. They lean on the trunks and hoods, and hammer—lightly—on the windows. Most drivers and passengers respond to the attacks in the spirit in which they're intended, screaming and laughing and seeming to genuinely enjoy themselves.

Eventually the throng is reassembled, and heads southwest, toward Washington Square Park. At the entrance, an old black man on a bike, a wide smile half-hidden by his long gray beard, cries out in a thick Jamaican accent, "Tripping! I'm f___ing tripping on LSD!"

The park is where most of the living walkers have been planning to finally join the horde. There were precious few to begin with, and they're quickly dispatched. The Red Sox fan gets his, and there are a few other isolated cases of brief, doomed resistance. The Zom-Be-Goners have long since lost their battle; their faces are green and hungry, and in the park they revel in the cannibalistic horrors with every bit as much gusto as their former prey. After all the willing victims have been converted, the zombies stand around for a while, laughing and swapping war stories as the sun goes down.

It's full dark by the time Sakmann leads the horde out of the park and east again, to the Continental, a bar on Third Ave. There's a zombie-themed concert down on Leonard Street at eight, but it requires ID, a subway ride, and twenty dollars. For many, the Continental will be the last stop.

It's a comfortable enough place to end up: ten shots for five dollars, the company of the kindred dead, and a very specialized kind of afterglow that can probably only be achieved through four or five hours of enthusiastic shambling. The dead have earned their rest. And they *need* their rest. Someday soon, they will have to rise, and walk again. In Paris; in Sydney; in Pittsburgh; in the capital of the world….

Conor Powers-Smith was born in Patterson, New Jersey and received his Bachelor's in Literature at Massachusetts College of Liberal Arts. He is currently working on his master's in Journalism at Quinnipiac University in Connecticut. He's been a horror fan since Nightmare on Elm Street 3 scared him out of about "a week's worth of sleep," and professes to be a big fan of zombie movies, especially Romero.

TAKE A BIG DRIPPING BITE OF THE ZOMBIE APOCALYPSE

Game Review

LEFT 4 DEAD

Valve Software
PC and XBox 360

So I'm limping down the alley, shotgun in hand, my three closest buddies right behind me, when a tongue whips down from the rooftop fifty feet above, wraps around my torso like a boa constrictor, and pins me to the wall. Then a hoodie-clad corpse appears at the end of the alley, covers the fifteen yards between us in one long froglike leap, and lands squarely on my chest. It rips into me, digging out big sloppy handfuls of flesh and flinging them in all directions. One of my buddies takes it down with his Uzi, and helps me up.

A hideously bloated zombie rushes us from behind. Someone puts a bullet in it, and it explodes—but it was too close. We're all splattered by the bile that gushes out, and now dozens of hunger-frenzied undead are converging on us. The safe room's just ahead, but we're in bad shape. We're low on ammo and fresh out of first aid kits, and I don't think we're going to make it this time.

This is more fun than it sounds.

Left 4 Dead, available for Xbox 360 and PC, is the latest in a wave of zombie video games released in the past few years, and it's among the best. Creepy, fast-paced and compulsively playable, *Left 4 Dead* delivers the blood-soaked chaos we've all come to expect from a zombie apocalypse.

You play one of four characters, thrown together by events and forced to work as a team for the sake of mutual survival. Get separated, and you won't last long; probably just long enough to watch some maggot-ridden corpse suck the marrow from your shattered femurs. Cooperation is everything. It's like Sesame Street, but with significantly more disemboweling.

The environments—an abandoned hospital, a ruined airport, a dilapidated farmhouse—are well executed, with plenty of dark corners and blind alleys for zombies to jump out of. Purists, be aware: these are your fast zombies. They run, they climb fences, they show great gusto. Think *Dawn of the Dead* remake; dozens of corpses streaming down an eerily-lit hallway, booking it like crazy toward their favorite food source. That would be you.

Then there are the mutant zombies: the Hunter, who pounces on his victims and rips them apart; the Smoker, who wraps people up with his impossibly long tongue; the Boomer, who vomits zombie-attracting bile; the Tank, a massive killing machine.

Campaign mode — you against the computer—is basically an introduction. The real show is online, in versus mode, where two teams go at it, alternating between survivors and zombies. So that kid that jumped me in the alley, and tore about ten pounds of meat off my ribcage? He's a human now, and I've got a big fat gut-full of zombie juice for him.

The city streets are alive with the dead. Four huddled human shapes are creeping out into the unknown. They have guns. They have each other. But I don't think they're going to make it this time.
— ***Conor Powers-Smith***

JOHN BRUNI
THE PATH

He gazed down the path lined with gnarled, dead trees and wondered if anything had ever survived here. There was an occasional weed, but the grass was wilted and brown. Not even moss grew between the ancient blocks of stone, set by the pilgrims when the Wild West meant Ohio. Why anyone would blaze a trail through such a wasteland was beyond Scott Emmett. Even as a child, he didn't care to know where the path led. His father had once warned him it was dangerous down there, not that young Scott ever intended to test the theory. Some told him there were bears, others haunts, and Scott continued not to care.

Except now it was *his* land, and if he was ever going to sell it—which was his intention, since the property was worth at least a couple million—he needed to see what he owned.

The inheritance had come as a complete surprise, as Scott was of the opinion that his father was too mean a bastard to die. He bore many scars that had been beaten into him by the old man, to say nothing of the undoubtedly true rumors of how his father had murdered his dear wife.

And now, much to Scott's pleasure, Edward Bradley Emmett was six feet under. Sleeping the Big Sleep. Worm chow. Chia corpse. The ground hogs were bringing him his mail. All these phrases, though old, brought a smile to Scott's face. Cancer, normally a hideous way to go, was amusing and ironic when it came to Old Mr. Emmett. He was a man who spent a good portion of his life sucking his supposed loved ones dry, and then his own body had devoured itself. Scott had a good, long laugh over that one.

THEY FOUND HER, DEAD AND NAKED, IN FARMER BROWN'S POND.

His humor was quickly killed by the hassle of dealing with lawyers, even if they'd already been paid for. Scott hadn't known how much red tape was involved when it came to dead folks, but he was starting to feel like he was wrapped in it, a disgruntled, crimson mummy. There was supposed to be a government agent coming to evaluate the land, but Scott wanted to see everything first, so there would be no surprises.

He glanced back at the house behind him. The Emmetts had been living there since they'd built it in 1699, and it resembled the castle they'd owned in England before moving to the colonies in a successful attempt to take advantage of the overseas demand for tobacco. The family had already been rich, but now they were walking moneybags, wealth built on the broken backs of countless slaves. Scott didn't mind the money, but the slaves sickened him. The idea that his ancestors owned human beings made him shiver and wonder what might be lurking in his own blood. Most times, he tried to ignore it. It wasn't as if *he* had done anything. And he'd never liked his family, anyway. But still, he felt guilty.

This was one of the reasons he hadn't even considered taking up residence at 517 Pawgnasauket Avenue. Looking at the artifice, one couldn't doubt its haunted nature, and if slaves had died here, they would make fearsome wraiths.

But there were also memories, none of which Scott felt like reliving.

(They found her, dead and naked, in Farmer Brown's pond.)

He took the first step down the decrepit path and marveled at how well the stones had been placed. Certainly there were cracks, but for the most part, the blocks were level. The going was easy; not once did he stumble as he walked down the slight hill into a small, muddy valley where a pond sometimes grew in the spring. His father had told him frogs hibernated in the ground until the water would come back, but Scott had never seen evidence of their existence, even after some digging committed when he was eight. It was the farthest he'd ever come down the path.

Until now. He crested the upward slope and found a forgotten forest, nothing but hollow, fallen logs and stumps. No animals frolicked, not even birds.

He continued down the path, wishing the sun would come out from behind the thick, gray clouds above. The weatherman had predicted rain, but the skies threatened with a storm, nonetheless. He doubted Apollo's bright gaze would make anything down here appear cheerful, anyway.

Beyond the trees, farther than he could have imagined, was the boundary of the Emmett land: a pair of rocky hills, beyond which

was a severe drop to the roiling sea seventy feet below. Scott had seen them on a map, but never in person. They resembled a woman's legs, their peaks her knees, and between them a cave.

When his father had kicked him out at age eighteen, Scott had moved to the city, where he'd stayed until now. Given his urban lifestyle, he'd never seen a cave before and had come to believe such things were created by pulp writers, despite pictures he'd seen in school books and on TV when he was a kid. As a result, he at once didn't believe his eyes, and suddenly desired to examine it closely. It was Something New and Mysterious. He wanted to know what was down there, and he truly hoped it was treasure. It looked like the kind of place a pirate would hide his booty, and it explained why his father had never wanted him to go down the path, as there were no dangerous animals around. The old man had been hiding his riches in the middle of nowhere, so the I.R.S. couldn't find it.

The sudden curiosity was so strong, he'd set foot inside the cave before practical questions came to him. It was dark, so why didn't he go back to get a flashlight? What about rope? Surely there were pitfalls. Maybe he needed to acquire a companion, as this wasn't a one man job. And what if something bad happened? What if the ceiling were to collapse and trap him?

(The autopsy said she drowned. Her lungs were full of water.)

Then, he saw the torch. It had burned recently. His father? Most likely. Scott reached into his shirt pocket and removed a pack of Camels and a lighter. He was trying to quit, but he found it a lot more difficult than he'd expected. He lit the cigarette first, then the torch. As the former burned slowly and provided a mere glow, the latter flamed brightly, illuminating the depths before him. The steady flicker revealed a set of natural stairs leading slightly downward. He heard a trickle of water from below, but the only thing he saw was rock, and a lot of it.

(They didn't know to check what kind of water it was, but it didn't matter; the neighbors knew what kind of man Mr. Emmett was, and they started the rumors accordingly.)

Scott started down, holding the torch in front of him, just in case a step had become too eroded to hold him up. *Wouldn't that be peachy?* he thought. *I'd break my neck and no one would ever find me.* His friends would ask questions, but he was certain they'd never discover him in time.

This thought did not deter him as he continued forward, eager for a flash of treasure, or whatever his father had hidden down here.

After what seemed like half an hour, Scott reached the bottom and soon wished he hadn't.

The floor was smooth, as if someone had sanded out any abrasions, sleek as the floor of the Capitol building. Several cold, dead torches lined the walls, and scattered about were contraptions made of splintered wood and dull metal. He cast his light among these things and was shocked to comprehend what they were.

HE KILLED HER. I KNOW BECAUSE I WATCHED IT HAPPEN.

(There were marks on her body, but they were not fatal. They knew Mr. Emmett's nature.)

A stretch rack. An iron maiden. A chair of spikes. Thumbscrews. Too many torture devices to notice at once, and they were not the tools of a dilettante dominatrix; they belonged in the days of the Inquisition.

Something tickled the back of Scott's mind. It felt like a forgotten memory trying to birth itself back into understanding, but it wouldn't come. Not yet.

Scott wasn't sure he wanted to remember.

He ran his fingers over the spiked seat to find every point still sharp but coated with flaking rust, or at least that's what he hoped it was. Nearby, shackles hung on the wall, showing a thick film on the inside of the manacles.

(Flesh was missing from her wrists, but interviews proved she'd always been that way.)

Scott's breath became heavier, and his heart beat faster, building its speed slowly like a well-rehearsed orchestra. The iceberg's tip was showing, and the rest was slowly coming to light.

Next to the shackles, he noticed a strange shape on the wall. It was black and lumpen, like nothing he'd ever seen before. The thought occurred to him it might be a large bat, but he knew it wasn't so. He'd watched many hours of Animal Planet with his friends and a bong, and he knew what a bat looked like.

When he got closer, he recognized it as some kind of cloak. He was about to reach out and grab it when it moved. Scott let out a gasp as he stumbled, striking the back of the spiked chair. It was bolted to the floor, so it didn't give an inch, forcing Scott forward to his knees. The torch slipped from his hands but did not go far. Fear drove him forward to scoop up the fire, and he pushed it out like a sword as the cloak fell away, showing a face both terrifying and familiar.

And it came to him.

He killed her. I know it because I watched it happen.

Scott remembered the fight. They'd thought he was in bed, but really he was in his father's library, reading a book of stories by some guy named Lovecraft. He'd heard them arguing in subdued tones, probably about money, which was usually the main topic of discussion. Their sounds instantly ceased with a *clang!* that reverberated throughout the house. Even as a child, he knew what it had meant, and he eased out toward the parlor, where he saw his father hovering with a frying pan over his unconscious mother. The old man giggled and dropped the utensil so he could take Mrs. Emmett up into his arms.

He took her down the path to the cave, and little Scott had followed. His treacherous mind had spliced it out like a damaged piece of film, and he'd never noticed the edit before. He *had* been down here, and because of the repression, he didn't know well enough not to come back.

Not to come back, and not to look once more into his father's pale, empty face.

"You're dead," Scott said, and though his fear was quite real, he felt silly saying it. The line belonged in a *Tales from the Crypt* comic book, except one where the moral didn't exist. What had he done to be placed helplessly in the hands of this lunatic again?

The face glared down at him, unmoving, like a statue made of flesh, but Scott knew it was a person. The eyes gleamed in the firelight, and the torso pumped with breath.

"I saw you in your coffin."

Still nothing, which was somehow worse than if Mr. Emmett had responded.

"What do you want?" Scott wailed.

Mr. Emmett stood silently, eyes blazing intently at his son.

"I'm not afraid of you!" His voice sounded false even to himself, not that it mattered. His words still had no effect.

FROM THE PAGES OF THE PAST

ISBN 9780970169914 $9.95

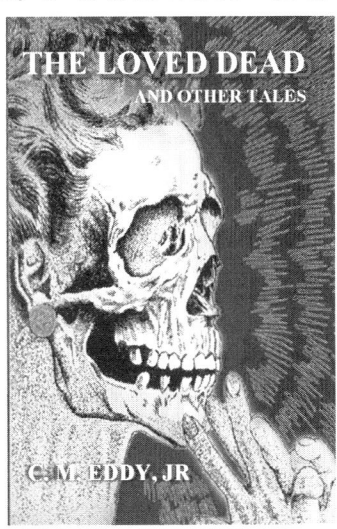

ISBN 9780970169921 $16.95

ISBN 9780970169907 $14.95

NEW COLLECTIONS FOR THE PRESENT

AVAILABLE WHEREVER BOOKS ARE SOLD

www.fenhampublishing.com

Scott willed himself not to shake. He was almost forty years old, far too old to fear his father. Too old to fear *anyone*. Gritting his teeth, he roared and pushed himself to his feet, lurching forward. With great satisfaction, he jammed the flames into his father's gut.

But it passed through him.

The torch hit the wall behind Mr. Emmett and splintered almost enough to extinguish. Panic flushed through Scott's system, but he quickly became calm as he realized what this meant: his father was a ghost, and years of reading old horror stories told him that ghosts could harm no one, unless the person in question had a heart condition.

Now that he was composed, Scott took down a fresh torch and lit it off the remains of the old one. He lifted it to the figure of his father and was unsettled to see the old man was still looking at him.

Can ghosts see the living? he wondered.

Finally, Mr. Emmett moved. He stepped forward among his torture devices, and a rich laugh emanated from his spectral vocal cords. It was soon overcome by a brittle shriek.

Scott saw his mother kneeling on the floor, naked, just like she was on that night so many years ago. Her arms were extended to the thumbscrews, where she was held in place. Her flabby, scarred breasts trembled as she watched her husband approach, holding a whip.

Scott wanted to turn away, but it felt like an external force was making him watch as his father lashed out at her time and again, her blood slapping the ceiling every time he drew back for another blow. She screamed, but no one could help her. The past was already written and could only echo throughout the eons.

Their ghostly images blinked out and reappeared at the rack. She was laid out and longer than she should have been. Bright pink stretch marks adorned her body, and in her mouth was a dirty metal funnel. Standing over her, legs spread, was her husband, and he was urinating into the cone. Her throat worked madly as she tried to swallow his waste rather than drown in it. When he was done, and she was still breathing, he laughed, jumping to the floor.

"My great-great-grandfather killed witches," Mr. Emmett said. "I've never met one, but if I ever did, I'd bring her here. For now, I'll have to be sated with a money-grubbing whore."

A lugubrious moan escaped from the funnel, but there was nothing that could be done. Mr. Emmett lifted a bucket and began to pour water down her esophagus. By the bottom of the stairs, Scott could see the image of a young boy, watching. It took him a moment to realize he was looking at his own ghost.

All the torches suddenly flared up, bathing the cave in light bright enough to have been provided by electricity. One by one, ghosts popped up at each torture device, and they were all the same. Scott remembered his father finding him. He remembered the rage. He remembered the pain.

At every different apparatus, all at the same time, he could see the torturer and the victim, his father and himself. Scott on the stretch rack where his mother had died. Scott in the iron maiden. Scott under the ever-dripping spout for days. Scott with weights crushing his legs. Scott with splinters under his fingernails. Scott inside a cage, in which it was too short to stand and too slender to sit. And more. So much more.

"No," he muttered, feeling the memories unfolding to him like nocturnal flowers. All his life, he remembered being beaten by his father, but never like this, yet it seemed right. This *really* happened to him, and it continued happening to the ghost of his childhood in this long-forgotten cave.

Scott could take it no longer; he fled up the stone steps and burst out the opening only to be confronted by yet another image of Edward Bradley Emmett. Scott's feet halted before the rest of him, and for a brief, terrifying moment, he thought he'd topple into this new haunt, but he managed to maintain his balance.

The ghost of his father never faltered; he remained as stoic in death as he had been in life. Even when torturing, killing and laughing, he was dull and empty.

Scott struggled for something to say, some invective to spit, or maybe a desperate plea for an apology that would never mean a thing. His tongue remained dry, though, and only a pant came forth.

"You can't leave, Scott," his dead father told him. "You're here with me forever."

These words broke Scott's paralysis. With a courageous yelp, he rushed forward to slip around his father. The old man-ghost put up a hand in his son's path, but it appeared to be a half-hearted attempt. Scott was forced to pass through it, as if the figure was only mist.

The weird sensation did not stop his flight. As he stumbled up the trail, he heard his father utter a laugh, amused by his son's fear.

It was only as he approached the house, exhausted and out of breath, that he realized he was still clutching the torch. Shaky, he brought the flames close to his face and blew them out with a tremendous breath.

For the next few days, he remained indoors, locked away from the world by TV he didn't care about and radio-broadcasted baseball games he couldn't pay attention to. His thoughts constantly revolved around the cave. At first, he thought he would simply never go down the path again and eventually the memory would fade, but time was Swiss-cheesing this theory until he knew in his heart it would never work. He considered hiring some guys from the city to seal the cave shut, and he'd almost called them several times, but something within him prevented this from happening.

On the seventh day, he figured out what this internal force was. For as long as he could remember, Scott felt like he was isolated from everyone else. Without love. Trapped in a purgatory of emptiness. His existence was meaningless. He was *soulless*.

> "YOU CAN'T LEAVE, SCOTT," HIS DEAD FATHER TOLD HIM. "YOU'RE HERE WITH ME FOREVER."

He'd thought his life had been stolen by his father's abuses, but he'd considered it only figuratively. Now he knew how literal reality was. His soul—his *ghost*—was being held captive in that cave, and to ignore it was to surrender any chance of happiness. The apparition of his father was right: he couldn't leave the cave. Not yet.

How could he free his innocence? An exorcist? Or will any man of God do? Scott didn't think so, as he'd never been a believer, and his father had never acknowledged a power higher than himself. He thought perhaps the occult could offer a spell, only that sounded too ridiculous to pursue.

There was a small part of him that constantly reminded him only crazy people saw ghosts, and maybe this was a problem for a shrink, one with a generous prescription pad. This voice, however, sounded false; in his heart of hearts, he *knew* the cave was truly haunted.

It then occurred to him that there were things on earth that *could not* have a soul. What if he destroyed the torture devices? Would it not seem that without those dread contraptions, the ghosts could not continue their never-ending cycle? The wooden parts would be easy to eliminate, but would it be enough to dent the metal bits?

The next day, Scott armed himself with a torch, a lighter and fluid, and a sledgehammer, and he proceeded down the path to end this once and for all. It was a sunless day, but the clouds weren't thick enough for rain. The wasteland was barren of life, as usual, but near the opening of the cave, he found a dandelion he hadn't noticed before. It wasn't the ideal life form, but it was something.

He leaned the sledgehammer against the hill so he could light the torch. When he was ready to descend, he gathered his equipment and entered the cave, for good or ill. As soon as he reached the bottom, he started lighting all the torches on the wall, expecting to see his father at every corner of the torture chamber.

The old man didn't show his face.

It was difficult to choose which device to destroy first, but as soon as he decided on the iron maiden, he didn't hesitate. Scott opened the case and brought the hammer down on each spike, one at a time. When the inside was rendered useless, he pounded the outside until it was an unidentifiable lump.

Next he broke out the wooden pieces of the spiked chair and threw them in a corner, where he would later use a torch to burn them. The rest, he pounded until it was just as ineffective as the iron maiden.

He moved from device to device, and still there was no sign of his father. Scott had expected resistance of some kind, but he had no trouble in breaking every single piece of equipment beyond repair. He stood, panting, watching the splintered pile of wood burn, still gripping the scuffed sledgehammer in both hands, trying to remember if he'd forgotten anything.

It came to him in a flash as bright as a mushroom cloud. *The shackles.* He whirled so quickly the sledgehammer dropped from his fingers and thumped to the floor. At first he went to scramble for it, but then he noticed how futile that would be.

Hanging from a pair of manacles was the transparent form of a young Scott Emmett. Standing next to him was his father, and he held the one instrument Scott had overlooked: the old man's fists. Mr. Emmett wrapped a hand around the child's throat.

"You thought you were being clever," his father said. "Not a bad plan. But torture devices don't kill people. People kill people."

"Don't do that," Scott said. "I'm begging you."

The old man smiled, but his eyes were blank. "I know. How does it feel to be a big, strong adult and still be at my mercy?"

"Just let me go. Please."

Edward squeezed suddenly and savagely. The child-ghost screamed, and Scott felt pain shoot through his throat. He fell to his knees, clutching the hurt spot, hoping to subdue the agony.

When he started flaking away, Scott knew there was no winning. His father was too cruel and ruthless, and pain like this never went away. Chips of Scott rained down from his writhing body and littered the floor like a layer of snow. His thoughts began fragmenting until he couldn't hold a cogent idea together. As his face opened, he felt his consciousness pour out like water from a broken jug. By the time his adult body had been reduced to dust, he was looking out from the eyes of his child-ghost.

"Welcome home, son," his father said, and with a powerful twist, he turned Scott's head around as easily as twisting the top off a jar.

Edward left his son's corpse hanging from the wall as he took a torch and started up the steps back to the real world. Before he reached the path, he carelessly stepped on the dandelion, severing the last life form of the wasteland from the ground without a thought. There it wilted, and soon it was gone.

John Bruni haunts Elmhurst, Illinois, where he likes to think he's a professional writer, as he tends to get paid for his work from time to time. With two hundred publications to his name, his recent work has appeared in *The Monsters Next Door*, *Lost Innocence*, *Cthulhu Sex Magazine*, *Detective Mystery Stories*, *The Nocturnal Lyric*, *Nuthouse*, *Night to Dawn*, and the paperback anthology, *Balance*.

John is also publisher of the horror, sci-fi and mystery magazine *Tabard Inn: Tales of Questionable Taste*, which can be found on the web at *www.talesofquestionabletaste.com*.

WEBLEY MARK VI REVOLVER

Compiled by Marie O'Regan

The Webley Revolver—called by some "the finest military revolver ever designed"—has become synonymous in the movies with the British Army during the early part of the 20th century. Its distinctive shape can be seen in such films as *Laurence of Arabia*, *Gunga Din*, and *The Four Feathers*; the Mark VI is even used, wrongly, in *Zulu*, set in 1887 when the Mark IV would have been in use. Even in non-war movies, the Webley was widely used (most notably as Indiana Jones' weapon of choice in *Indiana Jones and the Last Crusade* and *Indiana Jones and the Kingdom of the Crystal Skull*). T.E. Lawrence stated in his book *The Seven Pillars of Wisdom* that he used his "trusty Webley" to despatch Hamed the Moroccan, and that he also used it at the camel charge of Abu el Lissan, where he accidentally shot his *own* camel.

The Mark VI, otherwise known as "the ultimate Webley" .445 calibre six-shooter, was introduced as standard issue for British servicemen during World War I, on 24 May, 1915, superseding the Mark IV as the British Army's weapon of choice. The Mark VI was mass produced from 1915 to 1923, and was finally retired from use by the army in 1947.

On a practical level, the Webley Mark VI was known as a double-action top-breaking revolver (although it could also be thumb-cocked for deliberate shooting), with automatic extraction. This means that when the user breaks open the revolver (the hinge, or "break," being quite low down on the front end) in order to reload the weapon, any spent cartridges are automatically ejected from the cylinder, thus making reloading a simpler, faster process. The Mark VI, with a six-inch barrel and front sights, quickly showed itself to be a reliable and sturdy weapon, dealing admirably with the damp and muddy conditions in the trenches.

A range of accessories were soon developed, which included: the Prideaux Device—a speed loader device; a bayonet; and a special stock which allowed the revolver to be converted into a carbine (a longer muzzled weapon, but shorter and less powerful than a rifle), giving greater accuracy over longer ranges. These accessories weren't standard issue, and would only have been available for private purchase during World War I, predominantly by officers. Certainly the bayonet would have been impractical for everyday use—it was quite long, with a T-shaped cross section, and rendered the weapon off balance, thus reducing its accuracy and usefulness.

At the end of World War II, the Mark VI was declared obsolete, and replaced by the Enfield No.2 Mk I, by all accounts a vastly inferior weapon. It was still widely used by the British army during World War II, due to its popularity and reliability. Since the wars, large numbers of them have found their way to the U.S., where they are used to this day (often shaved down to accept .45 ACP and/or .45 Auto Rim cartridges), making the Webley Mark VI a true classic.

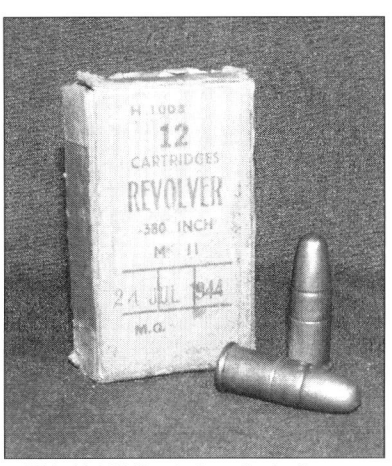

Webley Mark IV. Photo by Rama. Creative Commons. WWII dated .380" Revolver Mk IIz cartridges. Photo by Commander Zulu. Wikimedia Commons.

D.L. Snell's Market Scoops

The Market

The Magazine: Necrotic Tissue
Submission Guidelines: www.necrotictissue.com

Editor(s): Paige McCoy (interview with publisher Scott McCoy).

Pay rate: .01 cent a word + a Necrotic Tissue T-Shirt and .05 cents (Pro Pay) for the best story of each submission period.

Response Time: Four weeks.

Description: We are into horror, both speculative and psychological. We assume all stories submitted are fictional, so if they aren't, don't ever tell us. Any cross-over genres with a strong horror element will be considered. Dark humor, that is done well, (how is that for subjective?) is always appreciated.

NOTE: Horror author D.L. Snell conducted the following interview to give writers a better idea of what the editors of this specific market are seeking; however, most editors are open to ideas outside of the preferences discussed here, as long as they fit the basic submission guidelines.

The Scoop

1.) What authors do you enjoy and what is it about their writing that captivates you?

Until about two years ago, I had no idea how many quality small publishing houses there were. It still blows my mind how few people who love genre fiction are aware. My pat answer would have been King, Straub, Koontz and McCammon. I still love to read all of them, but I focus most of my book budget on Piccirilli, Keene, Waggoner, Tidhar and Russell.

Each writer is different in style and premise, yet they are all great storytellers who develop strong believable characters and put them in otherwise unbelievable situations. Even better, they sometimes create a character that shouldn't work and yet they make them seem normal.

I no longer have to wait months or years for my next horror fix with so many talented writers. Also, only within the last three years have I learned to appreciate short stories. I used to want only big ol' books that I could escape into for a few days, at least. I guess with age comes patience and an appreciation for variety.

2.) What are your favorite genres? Which of these genres would you like to see incorporated into submissions to this market?

I like all flavors of horror and sci-fi, but less and less fantasy. The first few "real" books I read as a child were fantasy, but there is a limit to how many unicorns I can handle.

I think fantasy is the hardest to blend into a horror story, or at least those stories appeal less to me than others. The beauty of horror is that it can darken any genre. Necrotic Tissue does like a good sci-fi/horror mix and also dark humor.

3.) What settings most intrigue you? Ordinary or exotic locales? Real or fantasy? Past, present, or future?

Ordinary settings made extraordinary appeal the most. A dangerous place, where one wrong turn can take you sideways to a nasty place. Present is the most comfortable for me and the easiest to pull off, but I'm a sucker for a story set in the past.

4.) Explain the type of pacing you enjoy, e.g. slow building to fast, fast throughout, etc.

I regularly claim to not be an action junkie, yet I continue to select stories that build a fast pace or are fast throughout. If it is done well, I really like a fast opening with a slightly slower middle to develop the character, then a race for the finish. This is hard to pull off and it is easy to flounder in the middle, but when done well, it's a great thing.

5.) What type of characters appeals to you the most? Any examples?

I'm a sucker for a regular person thrust into an unusual circumstance. It may sound cliché, but as a reader and a regular guy, I most associate with those characters. Also, since I have been through some unusual situations in the past, I prefer a character that has an edge and has an interesting history.

For a great story, it is important that the character take on the burden. There must be a choice against the darkness.

6.) What is your policy for vulgarity and sexual content?

Nothing too gratuitous, but if it is essential the story, then fine. We are not a young adult market; some of our stories are brutal, but with a purpose. The brutality or sexuality are not the story, but are integral to the plot or tone.

7.) Horror and violence can be blatant or suggestive. Which one do you prefer and why?

Do I have to choose? It may sound like a cop-out, but I prefer suggestive to build tension followed up with a double scoop of blatant.

8.) In fiction and in life, what do you find most horrific?

In fiction, it has to be situations in which there appears to be hope, but then that hope is dashed. So the stripping away of hope and the final realization that death is certain, but not yet arrived.

In life what I find most horrific is the possibility that I would die in a hospital bed after months of "treatment." The complete lack of control and, again, the slow diminishment of hope over time to an inevitable conclusion.

9.) In general, do you prefer downbeat or upbeat endings?

I have to go with upbeat. At the very least, I prefer good to triumph over evil. Of course, that can happen with a downbeat ending when the price is too high, but I can only take so many down endings at a time.

10.) What are the top three things submitters to this market should avoid?

1. Abuse. It's horror and some killing happens, but depictions of torturing children are a hard sell.

2. First person past tense stories where the protagonist dies at the end. I know this has been done by some well-known authors, but it irks me. If the story ends that way, go third person.

3. Unicorns. This is not a challenge, but I just can't picture a good horror story with unicorns in it, and yet I get at least one every submission period.

11.) What commonalities are among the stories you've rejected? Is there a particular aspect authors seem to get wrong?

Very slow beginning. If I hit page three and there is no sense of dread or building of tension, then I don't want it. Short stories need to grab the reader from the first paragraph preferably.

Dead horses. By this I mean, don't beat us over the head. I get a lot of stories where the writer uses six to ten paragraphs to describe in different ways that the antagonist or protagonist is bad, mean, smart etc. This goes beyond "show, don't tell"; you can over-show too.

12.) If you reject a story, how open are you to a revised version, or do you only want revisions upon request?

Rarely in the same submission period. If we think it is a good story that just needs some tweaking, we may say that. We don't ask for rewrites anymore, but we are willing to see one in our next submission period. If the story is really loose and we just disagree on a couple of points, we will send a conditional acceptance. If it needs overhauling to match our tastes, we want the writer to think about it before expending the effort. After all, the rewrite may still not work for us, but the original may work for several other markets. If we think the story is really well done and just not our style, we usually say that. We don't blow smoke; if we say that we mean it, and we hope the writer can find a home for it.

13.) Describe a story you've recently accepted or short-listed. What made it stand out from the slush pile?

The most recent story, and the last one we accepted for July's reading period (to be seen in April '09), was a well told flash piece with a cool premise. Interesting title, a nice hook in the first sentence and great execution. Usually I can tell by the third paragraph if it is going to be a great story. We don't accept them all, because some may not be right for NT, but I am rarely wrong about a great story.

14.) What trait are you seeking most in submissions to this market?

Courage. If you are going to tell a tale of horror, don't shy away from the premise that you have presented. The story must be true to itself, so if you are uncomfortable with the premise or the genre, write something you are comfortable with.

15.) Any last advice for submitters to this market?

Make sure your story is the right length. There are some 100-word premises, some 2,000, 5,000 and some that are novel length. One of the biggest mistakes we see are stories that are too condensed or too stretched for the premise.

For more scoops, go to *marketscoops.blogspot.com*.

Excerpt from...
Hiram Grange & the Chosen One
Kevin Lucia

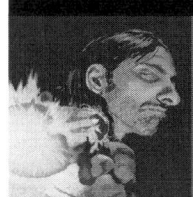

It was massive and quick, leaping and bouncing off coiled tentacles. Patches of its hide looked scorched. Bereft of its human husk, it moved quicker than its hybrid-brethren, though they lurched with frightening speed, also. Hiram waited for the right moment, aiming for the apex of its next bounce… and pulled the trigger. Thick tentacles lashed out and pushed off the wall. It launched away from his shot, which blew a useless, smoking hole in concrete.

Panning back across the hall, he pumped and fired; pumped and fired, gutting the hybrid Tanara'ri lumbering towards them. They exploded with muted, soggy roars. Flaming chunks of decayed flesh and necrotic tissue flew everywhere.

Hiram spun and tracked the adult Tanara'ri. It bounced off wall and floor, and then descended upon him with a shrill scream, tentacles lashing at his face. It closed the distance faster than he expected and slammed its rubbery, pulsating body into him. Both fell, the Tanara'ri on top, Hiram on the bottom, the Maruzen in the middle, jammed deep into the beast's gut.

Hiram flexed his finger against the trigger. The Tanara'ri squealed and tried to wriggle away, but it had impaled itself upon the shotgun. Its many eyes widened as it realized what would happen next.

"Sorry," Hiram crowed, "we're fresh out of helpless victims. Try again tomorrow, perhaps?" The beast keened. Hiram grinned and pulled the trigger.

The empty *clack* thundered. Both man and monster froze, considering the implications.

"Oh, *balls*," Hiram muttered. The rest of the shells were trapped beyond reach in his satchel, pinned between his back and the floor. There also was the remainder of his magnesium flares, along with his knife, trapped in its sheath.

The Tanara'ri understood Hiram's muttered curse. It blinked and rumpled with deep, wet laughter.

"Oh, really," Hiram snarled, "we'll see how funny it is, you sack of soggy shit..." Desperately rolling, he risked a one-handed grip on the Maruzen long enough to slip his right hand under his jacket to pull the Webley. Loaded with only standard slugs, perhaps if he hit the damn thing hard enough…

He jammed his father's gigantic black revolver into wet, stinking flesh and pulled the trigger, howling as the Webley boomed. The Tanara'ri shrieked and lurched. Ichor spurted everywhere. The odor of spent cartridges and burnt tissue filled his nose.

The Webley clicked empty on its sixth shot. The Tanara'ri shook itself, howled once more and pressed down. Hiram cursed and threw the Webley away. He grabbed the Maruzen with both hands as the thing bore down onto him, hissing in delight, tentacles lashing….

Light filled the hallway. A great wind blew and the room crackled with electricity. Every hair on Hiram's body stood on end. Waves of incandescent power pulsed outward, bathing he and the Tanara'ri in shining, blue-white light colder than anything he'd ever felt. The energy pushed into Hiram. It washed away all pain, regret, and stifled the buzz of the Hive mind. Deathly peace claimed him as he stared, eyes wide and unbelieving, jaw slack in amazement.

The Tanara'ri screeched.

Therese yanked the Tanara'ri off Hiram and held it high in the air. She pulsed with energy that swirled and crackled upon her skin; a living fire that could only be from one source: the Veil.

Even as Hiram stared at her, speechless, fear pricked him. Gazing into her face, he saw empty, inhuman features; cold, crackling cobalt blue eyes, devoid of remorse. Hiram knew a beautiful yet horrible truth: this was no longer Therese Ivanholde.

This was the chosen one of Mab's vision, and she was beautiful in her might.

The white river pulsed through Therese. It throbbed in tune with her heartbeat, pushed back the darkness, filled her with power. The fire was pure. It would cleanse all. It would purge, wash away, eradicate.

She was balance. The river flowed from her shining core, fed into the invisible fire flowing through all things. She saw multitudes, heard their voices, felt their tender caresses, warm embraces, but also endured curses, blows, violence and death.

She was light. *The light*, flowing and surging and being. She'd touched darkness, however, and hated it. The darkness must be destroyed. Everywhere it loomed. What it touched it ruined. Its hunger never ended. As she heard the psychic cries of joy from the multitudes, she wept in misery at the wailing shrieks of the forsaken.

There was no balance. There'd never been balance, not since life had first stuttered into being. There had always been darkness. It swelled, overcame, oppressed. She would destroy the darkness. She'd bathe the world in light, make it pure, clean…and empty. Of darkness, and everything else.

And she'd start *here*.

She squeezed, eliciting a wheezing cry from the Thing that made her soul hum. "Die," she whispered. With a nudge, she twisted the white river into It. Power surged and flowed into the dark thing. The beast howled as glowing cracks appeared in its hideous flesh. She filled it with fire; pure, white, empty fire.

It shuddered once, loosed a piercing wail. Then the fire burnt through, from the inside out. It exploded. Pieces of necrotic tissue, blazing with white-blue fire, flew everywhere, and then faded

> "She squeezed, eliciting a wheezing cry from the Thing that made her soul hum."

into mist, merging with the white river that pulsed out into the ether.

The darkness was gone. She'd made it pure. Peace settled over her, a sense of justice that Therese had never known before this moment.

Still–the world was dark, all around. It tugged at her senses. The thing's brethren still existed. Many surged towards them now. Therese flashed a feral smile. She'd destroy them, too, cleanse them, purge them of darkness. Once that was finished, the world would be next. The darkness must be purged, no matter where it hid. All must be purged with the white river, until everything was empty and pure.

Something *clicked*; a safety being flipped off. She turned and settled icy blue eyes on the man called Hiram. She smiled, pleased. In him, too, was darkness that needed purging. There was darkness, along with self-loathing. Despair. Hatred.

She stepped forward, hand raised. Hiram had done so much for her: saved her, risked his life for a stranger. The least she could do was give him peace, purge the darkness within him…even if that meant purging him as well. At least he'd have rest.

She reached out, the white river curling at her fingertips, and murmured, "Hiram…"

His face etched in pain, he raised his revolver and pointed it at her, finger tensed against the trigger. "I'm sorry, love. Please–just *don't* move."

She smiled wider. "Hiram," she cooed, "are you going to shoot me? Do you think you really can?"

He tipped his head, face still shadowed. "I don't know, love," he said, "but if you take another step closer, we might find out."

Her smile faded, cobalt eyes flashing a dangerous blue.

Hiram faced a cold, distant, powerful being. He kept the Webley trained on a spot between her eyes, finger tensed on the trigger. A buzzing alarm sounded in his head. More Tanara'ri were coming. They didn't have much time.

Which was fabulous, really. Quite splendid, because he had no fucking idea what to do next.

This cold, luminous woman with empty face and blazing eyes broke the impasse. "You have so much pain," she said, tonelessly. It was eerie; she sounded so much like Mab; her voice simmering with barely-restrained power. Visions of the horrible being Therese was destined to become rose in his mind, along with lands devastated by surging rivers of white fire. And of course, there was the image of him, throbbing with power: face blank, remorseless, burning with hatred.

What if this was the moment? Miles beneath the surface, amidst fire and destruction, with a horde of hell's hounds scrambling towards them, what if this was the crux upon which everything turned?

The thought's tempting, isn't it? Think of the things you could do with that power. Destroy evil, rid the world of darkness, bring back loved ones lost....I mean really, you could raise the blasted dead with that kind of power. Bring back Sadie and Mommy from the grave.

You wouldn't need the Dahlia at all...would you?

He pressed his lips, clenched his jaw. He'd never be able to control such power. He knew this. The frightening part? A large slice of him didn't care.

"So much pain, Hiram," she whispered, her cobalt eyes softening, "so much darkness." A smile cracked her features and though it looked genuine, it was still inhuman. "I could take that away; give you peace." In spite of the Webley, she took another step closer, clasped her hands behind her back. Tilting her head, she murmured, "I feel the darkness inside you. I can make that go away."

Hiram tightened his grip on the Webley; felt his stomach twist.

"I can help you," Therese insisted, "I can make you clean."

"Like you did with that Tanara'ri? No thanks, love. I'll keep my twitchy, dark quirks if it's all the same to you. Preferable to being atomized, you understand."

She shook her head with gentle – but superior - amusement. "I'd never do that to you, Hiram. Not after how you've helped me. I don't want to purge you, like the rest of the world needs to be purged. I just want to give you peace, make you clean and white inside…like me."

Hiram licked his lips. "Right. So here it is, then. 'Come to the dark side of the Force, Luke, etcetera, etcetera, taste the dark goodness of my power, it's like candy,' and all that, yeah?" He smiled. "Only in this case, its not the dark side but the white, self-righteous side. It's still the same thing." He paused. "You're not God, Therese. Darkness has its place. No matter how much power you have, you can't just run around eradicating it wherever you find it. Damn her tight little faerie ass, but Mab's right. It's all about balance; always has been, always will be."

A distant, wailing shriek echoed. He glanced over his shoulder, then back at Therese. "We haven't got time for this, love. More beasties are coming. We've got to duck and cover, find our way up to the surface, and send these tentacled bastards back where they came from. We can sort all this other shit out later."

She lifted her chin, expression haughty. "Why run and hide? Why send them back to the Abyss at all, when I can destroy them? You do the same thing."

Hiram shook his head. "No, it's different. I destroy their physical manifestations and send them back to the Abyss where they can't hurt people anymore."

Her smile was silken, seductive. "But they always come back, don't they?" She whispered. "They always come back, and then you have to do the whole thing, all over again. Why not destroy the Abyss; get rid of them all?"

Hiram froze. For a bare moment, nothing else existed. Not the Tanara'ri, not Bothwell, not the Confluence, or anything else…except for him, Therese, and her chilling words.

Why not? Think of all the lives that would be spared. No more Abyss or Abyss-bound.

It was maddening. He was so damn tired. All his days he spent drenched in some monster's guts, with blood on his hands. It was a rotten, dreadful existence. With no more Abyss, no more monsters…he wouldn't have to do it anymore.

The notion frightened the hell out of him, because not all monsters were made of necrotic tissue and conjured by dark magic. Destroying the Abyss wouldn't make monsters disappear.

Hiram shook his head. "You can't do that, Therese. You just can't."

She leaned forward. Her smile was cold, dismissive, and threatening. "Why not?"

Without realizing it, Hiram stepped backwards. He paused, sobering, his voice soft. "The Abyss exists for a reason, to maintain balance. That's what *I* do, love: fight for balance, hold the darkness at bay…not eradicate it. That's not my province. Besides, you can't *have* light without darkness, not in the corporeal world." He shook his head. "I've got no fucking idea how it works, but it does. You can't eliminate one without destroying the other. It's simply not for us to decide."

Her smile spread, cobalt blue eyes glowed. "But it could be."

Another shriek, closer this time. The distant pressure of the Hive pressed against his mind. He steadied the Webley, thumbed the hammer. "We're out of time. If there's anything of you left in there, Therese, back off. We can still do this the way it's supposed to be done. We finish this, we'll talk to Mab. She can teach you, train you, help you understand. Either way, you need to switch off the juice now, or I'll have to…"

"Kill me?" She raised white, frosty eyebrows. "Can you really kill me, Hiram Grange?"

He tried to ignore the growing drone of the Hive in his head. "If I do," he said between clenched teeth, "something horrible might *never* happen. The power inside you will go back to the Veil."

"Or so Mab says," Therese hissed. "Do you trust her?"

Hiram offered her a crooked grin. "Funny thing about that; I do. That's the odd thing about the faerie. They're bound to the universe's order."

"So you'd preserve the Abyss…even if that means you'll go there, someday?"

Hiram swallowed. This was it, wasn't it? That damned moment of truth everyone thought so highly of? As far as Hiram was concerned, the whole thing sucked balls.

"Yeah," he rasped, "I would."

She straightened, her face stiff. "Do it, then. Shoot me. Kill me, now."

He blinked. Her face flushed with anger and something else – perhaps fear, even while holding all this power - she yelled, "Do it now!"

Hiram froze. His heart pounded. He looked into her eyes and saw the real Therese merging with this powerful construct, if only for a moment. When she screamed, it was *her* voice, and not one of a demagogue rising. "Please, Hiram – it's the only way! Do what you have to!"

The Hive thundered in his head. Sweat poured down his face. The

Tanara'ri screamed in his mind, so much closer. His finger pulled the trigger back…

"Damn!" he whispered, voice cracking, "damn it all to hell!"

He couldn't do it.

Therese flickered and her aura faded. "H-Hiram," she whispered, eyes shifting between cobalt orbs and human irises, "w-what's happening? What's happening to me?"

The light faded and vanished. Therese's eyes reeled back into her head and she collapsed, a limp rag doll. As she fell, Hiram's head filled with the Hive's drone. The halls echoed with screams and the slithering sounds of tentacles on walls and floors.

Somehow, Hiram managed to catch Therese in the crook of the arm holding the Webley. Cradling the unconscious girl, spinning to face the hell that scrambled towards him, Hiram raised the Maruzen and filled the hallway with fire and his own hoarse yells.

**To be continued in
*Hiram Grange
& the Chosen One*....**

Kevin Lucia is a Contributing Editor to *Shroud* Magazine. His short fiction has appeared in *Coach's Midnight Diner*, Shroud's *Abominations* and *Northern Haunts*, Snuff Book's *RAW: Brutality as Art*, and Necrotic Tissues' *Malpractice: An Anthology of Bedside Terror*. His short story "Monsters" will appear in a forthcoming issue of *All Hallows Magazine*. "Way Station", his first short story, was awarded Editor's Choice honors in *Midnight Diner*, and was selected for *The Relief Journal's Best of 2007* edition. He's currently finishing his MA in Creative Writing and teaches high school English. For updates via free newsletter, send a blank email to newsletter@kevinlucia.net, or visit him at: *www.kevinlucia.net*.

STEVE VERNON'S
HAUNTINGS, FREAKS AND MYSTERIES
THE CADBOROSAURUS CARAMILK SECRET

There you are, twelve-year-old Frank Stannard, out with your friends for a salt water canoe excursion into the Northern British Columbia Pacific—just handy to Cadboro Bay. Suddenly you're eye to eye with a sea serpent. Five canoes worth of cold Cadborosaurian flesh. The beast rears up out of the water and stares down into Frank's canoe.

"I bet you I can hit it," Frank says.

Just that quickly young Frank unpockets his slingshot and wings a stone straight at the brute. The stone kapwings off of the creature's bony forehead.

Frank has just enough time for an instantaneous transcendental moment of oh-shit-I-can't-believe-I-did-that.

"Paddle!" he shouts.

He and his friends turn their canoes and make it to the shore. The sea serpent lowers into the ocean like a cobra returning to its basket. No one was harmed in the making of this anecdote, but I'll bet you a solid chocolate Hershey bar that several of those boys required a hasty change of drawers.

Steve Vernon

HE WHO WRIGGLES

Like most of Canada's best kept secrets, the natives had known about Cadborosaurus years before white men first got wind of it. The Manhousat tribe called it hiyitl'iik which translates as "he who wriggles." The Comox tribe called it Naumkse-le kwala or "the sea monster."

What ever you call it folks have been spotting these beasts off the BC coastline for decades. The sightings are abundant and all seem to have the same basic description in common. The beast looks like a serpent with a humping back, a horse-like head, a long neck, and a pair of large webbed hind flippers that form a fan-like tail behind.

On October 5, 1933, two yachtsmen on two individual yachts spotted the beast at two different times. The New York Herald Tribune picked up the story from the Victoria Daily Times and Cadborosaurus was officially acknowledged.

THE TRAIL

1905 • Two lumberjacks are chased by a creature with a head like a giraffe and two small five inch horns on its head.

1922 • Two lighthouse keepers saw what they thought was an approaching ship but turned out to be a Cadborosaurus.

1932 • Novelist Hubert Evans reports seeing a sea serpent with a long snaking body undulating in a series of bumps and a horse-like head with nostrils and either ears and/or horns.

1932 • That same year a family of three spotted a creature in the BC waters. It was over 60 feet long, at least 5 feet thick, with a bluish-green hide that shone in the sun like aluminum.

1937 • Whale flensers discover the carcass of a strange serpentine-like beast with a camel-like head. Photographs are taken but the carcass is lost to decay.

1991 • Phyllis Harsh of John's Island, BC insists that she returned a beached baby Cadborosaurus to the welcoming waters of the Pacific.

1996 • In the Amphipacifica Journal of Systematic Biology, Drs. Paul H. LeBlond and Edward L. Bousfield officially recognize the Cardborosaurus as a separate and unique species. Bousfield and LeBlond believe the historical records about this creature contain sufficient evidence of "specimens in hand" to conclude "the animal is real and merits formal taxonomic description."

1998 • Saltspring Island fishermen catch what they believe to be the carcass of an authentic Cadborosaurus. Fearful of contaminating their commercial catch they dump the carcass overboard.

2006 • The beast was spotted just 40 metres offshore, raising its head and exposing its distinctive finned tail.

GRIMOIRES & TOMES
BOOK REVIEWS

COVENANT
John Everson
Leisure Fiction

With his wonderfully frightening mass market debut, John Everson cuts a bloody swathe through our imaginations with *Covenant*. His chilling tale isn't all blood and gore, however. Everson writes with deft skill, leading readers into what seems to be only a well-told suspense/thriller. By the novel's end, however, Everson unleashes his hellish vision with a vengeance. Readers will be captivated—and horrified—until the final page.

Small-town reporter Joe Kiernan is aching for a good story, something big, worthwhile. Since leaving his high profile job at the *Chicago Tribune*, he's been hiding out, trying to bury memories of one story that hit too close to home. Reporting on the mundane intricacies of small-town life is wearing thin, though, and Joe's itching for a story with substance.

When a local teen takes a fatal leap from Terrel's Peak, the cliffs outside town, Joe's instincts flare up. Despite pressure from authorities and his editor to leave the story alone, he starts sniffing around, sensing a story larger than any he's ever worked before. Before long, he uncovers a string of suicides dating back several years. As he digs deeper into town history, Joe discovers a horrible pact made with an awful force. Something terrible dwells in the hollows of Terrel's Peak, and because he's ignored everyone's advice, Joe has blundered directly into its path.

Covenant is a chilling novel that runs the horror spectrum. Everson sets up his story well, fleshes out Joe Kiernan as a character readers can root for, and truly sets him against a pitiless, horrible evil. Better yet, in an excerpt from his next novel, *Sacrifice*, readers are offered a peek into Joe's future, promising a recurring character in a horror series that's sure to draw a healthy fan base for years to come. — ***Kevin Lucia***

Visit www.johneverson.com and www.myspace.com/johneverson.

CRIMSON
Gord Rollo
Leisure Books

Last year, Gord Rollo debuted with his first novel *The Jigsaw Man* and established himself as a premier voice in horror fiction. Though his follow-up effort *Crimson* lacks some of Jigsaw's emotional punch, it's still a frightening ride. His voice is strong and he continues to frighten and entertain. The novel begins with a jolt: an unthinkable, bloody act, and then settles into a haunting tale that ends with a twist.

From the moment Johnny moved to Dunnville, he and Pete, Tommy and David were best of friends. They hung out, talked about "guy stuff" and did things that boys do. The only problem? Johnny and his mother moved into Old Man Harrison's place; an

GRIMOIRES & TOMES

old house haunted by the legend of a man who murdered his whole family. They avoid playing there for awhile, but a Saturday afternoon outing is inevitable.

What they find is unspeakable evil. A being of incalculable malice has slept in an old well since the horrible day of Old Man Harrison's slaughter. All this time, it's been waiting for new flesh to play with. When Johnny and his friends accidentally disturb its underwater sleep, they're exposed to an evil that will torment them for the rest of their days.

In many ways, *Crimson* displays Gordo's versatility. While *The Jigsaw Man* offered wrenching questions about quality of life, *Crimson* is a classic tale that never loses its strength: how timeless evil follows unfortunate souls and dominates their destiny. His characterization of four boys faced with a horror their parents dismiss is authentic, and he doesn't take this novel to its expected "childhood friends band together to destroy evil" conclusion.

A few reviews may be overly enthusiastic, however. One claims "*Crimson* is [Stephen King's] *It*'s superior in every possible way." This isn't quite accurate, because Crimson doesn't have the same depth as *It*... but then again, what recent novel does? Aside from that, Gord Rollo's second outing is perfect to curl up with on late, cold winter nights. It'll make you wonder what's hiding at the bottom of your well. — **Kevin Lucia**

Visit www.gordrollo.com and www.myspace.com/gordrollo.

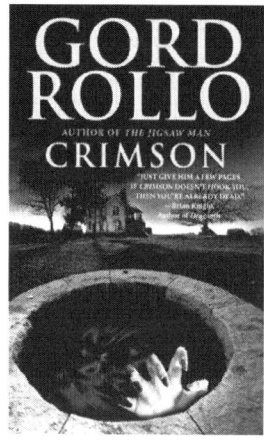

DARK HOLLOW & GHOST WALK

Brian Keene
Leisure Fiction

Dark Hollow and *Ghost Walk* are bookend novels, pivotal works in the Brian Keene universe. In both, Keene continues to expand his mythos, as well as expound upon the metaphysical. Author Adam Senft (*Dark Hollow*) is a tragic hero, a man who only wants to protect his wife, but commits the ultimate hubris when pushed too far. Keene plumbs spiritual depths in character Levi Stolzfus (*Ghost Walk*), a man determined to serve God as best he can, battling forces beyond his understanding. Both works show Keene at his best, and his growing story arc network lays a foundation for the most intriguing mythos since Stephen King's *Dark Tower* series.

When successful midlist author Adam Senft takes his dog Big Steve on a walk in the woods near LeHorn's Hollow, all he wants is a break from writing. Everything changes that day, however, when he hears ghostly pipe music drifting from the woods' dark depths, and sees something he can't understand or explain. Soon after, neighborhood women begin disappearing, lured into the woods by an ancient spell they can't resist. Desperate to protect his wife (who still mourns the loss of their unborn child) and his friends' wives, Adam delves into dark magic and the cursed history of LeHorn's Hollow for answers. What he finds could very well lead to their salvation… or his own destruction.

A year later, evil has returned to LeHorn's Hollow. Levi Stolzfus is a man of convictions; so much so he's been exiled from his fellow brethren and faith community. Undaunted, Levi continues serving God in his way, remaining true to his calling. One night, Levi encounters something evil, alien to this world and outside God's provision.

BOOK REVIEWS

Driven by this dark encounter, Levi joins forces with frustrated small town journalist Maria Nasr and learns of a Halloween attraction opening near LeHorn's Hollow. He's gripped by the terrible premonition that evil stalks the gates of our world, waiting for the right moment to usher in our destruction.

He'll need all his arcane knowledge and every ounce of strength to face what's coming, but that alone isn't enough. One thing remains; the center lynchpin to everything: a man convicted of a horrible crime and committed to a mental institution, former midlist author Adam Senft.

Both works mix impressive complexity with gut-wrenching trauma and chilling moments. Keene effortlessly blends religion with philosophy; even sprinkling in Lovecraftian lore for good measure. Through these two novels, Keene's "Labyrinth Mythos" grows and connects with many of his other novels, opening speculation as to how and when he'll craft another chapter of the Labyrinth tale. — *Kevin Lucia*

Visit www.briankeene.com and www.myspace.com/brian_keene.

FROZEN BLOOD
Joel A. Sutherland

This is old-school horror, the kind of book that you might have seen back in the 1980s. It's straightforward, no-frills, no hidden meaning, scary atmospheric stuff. Its set-up is old school too.

Two estranged sisters are coming back into each other's lives due to the recent death of their father, and the reading of his will, taking place in his mansion near Ottawa during a severe and seemingly never-ending hailstorm.

There is a great deal of mistrust between the two. Tara is a recovering alcoholic. Her relationship with sister Evelyn was destroyed following the death of Evelyn's daughter—killed by a drunk driver—an act her sister symbolically identifies with Tara herself. Before the evening described in the book the two had not communicated in three years.

There's even the kind of twist you would get in many 1980s horrors. After about sixty or so pages everything points to a battle between the two sisters—each descending into their own brand of madness—and heaven help anyone who gets in the way.

However, things change. The storm, initially seeming to be the device used to keep the sisters locked together in the family home, claims its first (in these pages at least) victim when the lawyer attempts to leave. The ice pellets of the hailstorm tear at his skin, beating him unconscious to the ground and reducing him to a bloody pulp.

But this is not a book that relies on shock. Even with the lawyer's death you'll find no detailed descriptions of gore. The author is going for atmospheric fears, using the isolating power of a serious storm to unsettle. There are no demons, no mysterious strangers, witchcraft or magicks here.

The ghosts Tara sees and interacts with regularly could be a result of her mind. There is no conclusive proof they actually exist. Even the mysteries (the off-screen alterations to the contents of the house) are in essence mundane, much more likely the result of malevolence on one sister's part, or madness on the other.

This book works best in the way it gradually increases your knowledge of the sisters' relationship through Tara's flashbacks and conversations with the dead. The initial sense of incompleteness may seem a little confusing, but this slow peeling back of the layers gives you each new piece of information at just the right moment—when its affect is greatest.

GRIMOIRES & TOMES

In many ways the familiar big-old-house setting, sibling rivalry and deeply flawed main characters work for him. He's not wasting time describing the background. We know it and he knows we know it. It allows him to get on with it—to tell us a story.

Sutherland is not the finished article by any means. His descriptions are occasionally prosaic when they could make the scene more real. Some of the jumps are too abrupt, the dialog a little stiff. But his pacing is good, and he presents an ending that doesn't wimp out. His ability to spin a good yarn, with just the right creepiness-factor, makes this a very entertaining debut novel. — *I.E. Lester*

JAKE'S WAKE

John Skipp &
Cody Goodfellow

Jake Calloway is a preacher—although not your holier-than-thou type. He's a con man, very charismatic but a total fake. He's also not a man for abstinence, for achieving a spiritual bliss by avoiding sin. Drugs, alcohol, hookers, you name it—Pastor Jake is determined to get his fill. Or rather, he was.

His latest sexual conquest has gone a little awry. As he did many times before, Jake picked up a young woman in a bar and headed back to her place. Problem for him was, in the middle of the sex her boyfriend arrived home and killed Jake. But it's not the end of Jake's story.

Jake's widow Esther and members of his congregation have gathered at her family home for a wake, a chance to express their grief. Or, in some cases, their relief. Jake walking in, a shambling rotting corpse, is the last thing they expect. And, unfortunately for them, Jake seems to have acquired superhuman strength in the bargain—and is very much intent on using it to kill every single person attending.

As horror goes this isn't subtle. If you want your horror to be moody, character-driven drama with a gradually rising undercurrent of spookiness you're in the wrong place. Skipp and Goodfellow are more from the "I'm going to rip out your lungs with a metal hook" stable of horror. They get bloody—very bloody—and they don't keep you waiting long.

But don't think for a second that this is just dismemberment following disemboweling following decapitation. This isn't just gore for the sake of it. There is a story, and even though you think the odds are stacked heavily against the wake's attendees, you feel some of them might just survive—might overcome the bad guys.

This is not a book where you will encounter those fuzzy grey areas of horror (dark fantasy, in other words). Here the bad guys aren't going to agonise about some of the things they've done, or fight their natures to become better people. Jake and his cronies relish the kill, they glory in the gore. These guys are evil, pure and simple. And they like it.

This is horror that is willing to stick its head up and admit to the fact. Damn good job, too! My hat's off to you, Messrs Skipp and Goodfellow. — *I.E. Lester*

JOHNNY GRUESOME

Gregory Lamberson

Johnny Grissom (or Gruesome) is a teenage misfit, malcontent and struggling his way through High School. Okay, "is" is perhaps not the best word, as very soon after the start of this book he flips out and is killed in a fight with a friend. However, Johnny does not want to let things lie.

Through sheer strength of will Johnny rejects the pull to go into the light, and returns to his corpse determined to get revenge on a world he feels has treated him badly. And so, having learned how to animate his dead and embalmed body, he begins killing.

A lot of books, films and TV shows of the last few years have seen the reader or viewer getting inside the mind of the monster. Since Anne Rice's *Interview with the Vampire* was released it has become quite the vogue. The problem is this can have the effect of watering down the horror.

If you like reading a romance tale with a bit of a dark edge then this is not a bad thing. But for all of us who just like horror it has somewhat diluted the field. Gregory Lamberson, though, has bucked this trend. This book may take you inside the mind of the monster, but it doesn't let up on the horror at all by doing so.

Just because you understand Johnny Gruesome's reasoning behind his activities, doesn't make this any less horrific. In fact, reading the thoughts of a shambling decomposing corpse, and knowing his feelings over his body slowly falling apart, ramps up the horror quotient.

The book is a fantastic homage to 1980s pulp style horror. Johnny Gruesome is made from the same kind of antihero, horror bad guy mould as Freddy Krueger. Yes, he is committing some pretty horrendous crimes, but part of you wants his path of destruction go on and on.

Eric Carter, Johnny's former best friend turned target-for-death, is a wonderful character. He reads like a male version of the Jamie Lee Curtis role in Halloween - a bit nerdy but basically okay, and with hidden strengths. Then to this mix Lamberson adds in all the expected supporting characters. We have jocks; the school newspaper reporter; a sympathetic young female teacher (perfect wet-dream fodder for the high school males); her cop husband investigating the killings; Johnny's alcoholic father; etc, etc, etc.

Lamberson has the balance just right. This book has horror components (shambling decaying corpse, frequent brutal killings) but it doesn't overdo them. He hasn't written a series of gory set pieces loosely strung together with a second-rate plot. This story is well paced and has one or two moments of real suspense, and even a surprise or two.

This is a book that pushes all the right buttons—mostly with a bloody stump of a finger. Great stuff! — *I.E. Lester*

SHEEP & WOLVES

Jeremy C. Shipp
Raw Dog Screaming Press

Jeremy C. Shipp has established himself as a new, haunting voice in dark fiction. With the release of his first collection of mind-bending, spine-tingling (perhaps gut-wrenching) stories, Shipp solidifies his growing reputation. He'll make you laugh, scream and cry... perhaps all at once.

Shipp's work boasts an insane mix of intelligence, social astuteness, dark imagination, and perhaps even clever dementia. Over the years, many writers have imitated this "bizzaro-style" of first and second person narration with limited success. Shipp sidesteps these clichés by tugging his stories in surprising directions. Embedded inside these twisted tales are nuggets of social awareness that lift them above the realms of mere shock value.

Some of the best stories seize hold of genre conventions and flip them. In "Those Below," Shipp employs the age-old zombie vehicle, albeit with a twist. In "Camp," young boys are sent away to a different type of summer camp for an awful sort of training, with disastrous results.

GRIMOIRES & TOMES

In "Baby Edward," a man's internal conflict is given flesh in the most bizarre of ways. "The Rules" is a quick, bloody slash at zealous righteousness, while "American Sheep" enslaves an unwilling participant in a literal corporate machine.

Many of these stories will be not completely understood, but that's part of the insane fun of Jeremy C. Shipp. Sometimes you'll only glimpse the truth from the corner of your eye...but that'll be enough to change the way you think for days to come.
— *Kevin Lucia*

Visit www.jeremycshipp.com and www.myspace.com/jeremywriter.

Shroud Publishing and Norman Rubenstein humbly request that you help wounded service people in their transition back to their lives and families.

Whatever your stance on the war in Iraq is, and regardless of your political affiliation, we ask that you take a moment and visit the Wounded Warrior Project web site to see how you can help those that have made the ultimate sacrifice for our country.

WWW.WOUNDEDWARRIORPROJECT.ORG

SUCCULENT PREY
Wrath James White

Ten-year-old Joey Miles was kidnapped, repeatedly raped, and stabbed more than a dozen times before his captor dumped him in a park. He was the lucky one—the first victim of a serial child-killer, the only one of his victims to survive.

The adult Joseph Miles is a gian—six-and-a-half feet of muscle and intensity—often likened to Superman. He is also a driven man—addicted to sex, he has cannibalistic fantasies. He is also an intelligent man, trying to deny his more violent urges and understand what makes him the way he is.

An encounter begun in a sex-club causes him to take the first step in what he sees as an inevitable progression in serial murders. Believing he is infected with a killer virus, he decides to seek a cure, a way of allowing him to live a normal life—with the woman he has just mutilated.

BOOK REVIEWS

Wrath James White has managed to do the impossible. He's managed to write something that I found disturbing. It's impressive after three decades of reading horror fiction. And he's done by making it very, very human—only the worst aspects of humanity.

Using serial killers as the focus of horror stories is nothing new. A moment's thought brings to mind Hannibal Lector, Michael Myers, Jason Voorhees and Freddy Krueger—and they form only the very tip of a very large blood-stained iceberg.

But none of these have gone as far out there into the visceral as White does here. The plot itself is a little unoriginal. The concept of a surviving victim of a serial killer himself becoming a killer is very familiar and somewhat overused. But here it does not matter. It's the excessive violence of Joseph Miles' acts—portrayed so vividly you feel you are as covered in the gore as he is—and the rationality of his belief in a cure that keeps your attention. This is a book, once started, that you have to keep reading.

And this is where the author's skill is most apparent. He's created a book this incredibly violent without sacrificing plot. This isn't a loosely strung together series of brutal acts. Miles may be a psychopath (to say the least) but he has a purpose. When he gives in to the urges he does it largely on his terms. He allows his beast limited reign to stop it consuming him totally—rationalising each incident as necessary if he is to remain in control long enough to find his cure.

This book is likely to prove too gory and violent for some readers, even some long-term horror readers. Be warned, if you prefer your horror to be the spooky kind—an underlying dread, almost PG-13 level, rather than out and out flesh-ripping, you really should steer clear.

But if you are a gorefiend, like me, this should definitely be on your reading list. — *I.E. Lester*

> Shroud is interested in reviewing published works of dark speculative fiction.
>
> Please send advance review copies at least one month before publication date, accompanied by appropriate press materials. Shroud is also available for jacket blurbs provided that the content is sent well-enough in advance.
>
> Other books can be sent at any time with the understanding that we cannot guarantee that we will review everything and review materials cannot be returned. Sorry!
>
> Send review materials (Books, DVDs, Games, CDs) to:
>
> **Shroud Publishing**
> **121 Mason Rd.**
> **Milton, NH   03851**
>
> Questions?
> editor@shroudmagazine.com

progknostications
BY MICHAEL KNOST

When Tim asked me to write a column for *Shroud*, we kicked around a number of concepts before settling on his idea of focusing each piece on an outstanding up-and-comer in the horror genre, followed by an original story by the chosen author.

The first person that came to mind for this feature was Nate Southard.

I met Nate a few years ago at Camp Necon and found him to be personable, humorous, and professional. After reading a few of his stories, I asked Nate to write a tale for *Legends of the Mountain State 2*. If you've read anything by him, you know what I mean when I say he has the goods.

As a voracious reader, it was only a matter of time before young Nate started writing. One of his earliest influences was his older brother Mark, who wrote a satirical column (set in the fictional Indiana town of Mud Hollow) for the local paper. "The column was, at various times, thoughtful, hilarious or heartbreaking," Nate recalls. "I was mystified by both Mark's writing and his ability to create an entire world."

Other influences were Robert McCammon, Clive Barker and Stephen King, although he spent most of his time reading comic books. "Chris Claremont and Alan Moore were my heroes," Nate admitted. "Looking back now, I only cringe about the Claremont part."

Nate later moved to Austin, Texas to study screenwriting at the University of Texas, where he discovered Warren Ellis, Andrew Vachss, Richard Laymon, Jack Ketchum and Bentley Little. "Doing research on these writers opened my eyes to the small press and everything that was going on there."

Frequency Press published his first graphic novel, *Drive*, in 2005. A trip to Rundberg followed in November of the same year. "I was trying to get blurbs for *Drive*, and I sent a copy to Brian Keene right around the same time he selected my short story 'Digging' for *Horrorfind.com*. He really started to champion my work, and he's been my cherished mentor and friend ever since." In 2006, the two collaborated on the graphic novel version of Brian Keene's *FEAR*.

"Nate reminds me of me," Keene recently stated. "The me from a decade ago, who was just getting started in this business—except that Nate has more talent and more common sense than I did. There are a lot of exciting up-and-comers, but I really think Nate is the one to watch. He's serious about the craft. He doesn't waste his time jerk-

New Blood: Nate Southard

ing off on the Shocklines message board or trying to change HWA because he understands that none of these will make him a better writer. Instead, he sits his ass down in a chair and writes. And that's what it takes."

Brian is not the only well known author to have taken part in helping Nate grow as a writer and professional. Norman Partridge, Jim Moore, Greg Gifune and Christopher Golden are just a few that have made an impact in his career as well.

"I've known Nate for just a couple of years," Golden said. "He's a talented writer with a take-no-prisoners writing style that ought to earn him legions of fans. Even better, he strikes me as a good guy, thoughtful and professional, and when you combine those things with skill and a purity of ambition, you've got all the elements needed for a breakout success. I hope it comes his way."

Michael McBride was a fellow workshopper at the Borderlands Writer's Bootcamp in 2006 and remembers Nate asking him a few weeks later if he would read a novella he was working on entitled *Run Like Hell*. "I don't know what I expected, but the story blew me away," McBride remembers. "It was right up there with the best of Ketchum's work." Michael put Nate in touch with Paul Goblirsch, founder of Thunderstorm Books, and from that introduction, *Run* was reborn as *Just Like Hell*, which sold out almost as quickly as it hit bookshelves in 2008.

One of the things I like about Nate is his appreciative nature in pointing out the people who have helped him during his writing career. "I owe a great deal to my first readers: Kelli Dunlap and my girlfriend Shawna," he admits. "I'd churn out nothing but garbage if not for them."

If you would like to find out more about Nate Southard, visit his website at www.NateSouthard.com.

In the meantime, sit back and enjoy Nate's story "Inside the Box."

Nate Southard Bibliography

Books

Broken Skin
Short Story Collection.
Thunderstorm Books. Due July 2009.

Just Like Hell
Thunderstorm Books. 2008.

Select Short Stories

"Captain Jinkies"
Dark Recesses Press. 2008.

"Another Lonesome Day"
Bits of the Dead. 2008.

"For Just One Night"
Legends of the Mountain State 2. 2008.

"Scenic Pastures"
A New Dawn. 2008.

"Of Cabbages and Kings"
The Dead Walk Again! 2007.

"Insomnia Is My Only Friend"
Horror Literature Quarterly #1. 2007.

"Rain Against My Window"
Gods and Monsters. 2006.

"Silent Corners"
Trunk Stories #3. 2005.

"A Team-Building Exercise"
Aoife's Kiss. 2005.

"The House on Toledo Street"
Wicked Karnival #6. 2005.

"Digging"
Thirteen Vol. 1 Issue 10. 2004.

"Hell Inside"
Horrorfind.com. 2004.

Graphic Novels

Brian Keene's *FEAR*
Frequency Press. 2006.

Drive
Frequency Press. 2005.

A Trip to Rundberg
Frequency Press. 2005.

NATE SOUTHARD
INSIDE THE BOX

The old man cried out again. He kept screaming about the pain in his belly. He'd been complaining about his stomach since the trip began. Over time, he had only managed to increase the volume of his cries. The other stowaways ignored him. The man was hungry, nothing more.

Yingjie sat in the corner of the big metal box, trying to ignore his own hunger pains. All around him, the others wailed, their sobs almost as loud as the old man's. It had been five days since their arrival, since they'd been taken from the boat, and the man who was supposed to let them out hadn't come. Where was he? Why hadn't he arrived and set them free? He was supposed to spirit them all away to begin their new lives in America. Surely he hadn't forgotten them. Where was he?

Yingjie pushed the questions aside and tried to sleep through the screams of others. It wasn't easy, but after many hours he managed the task.

He dreamed of sunlight and of his mother. She looked down at him, tears in her eyes, as she guided him into the metal box. She told him how life would be better in America, how she would join him soon. Then, workers shut the cargo container, and the world went dark again.

He woke to the sound of sobs. A woman was blubbering that her baby had died. He wanted to care, but couldn't. There were more important things to worry about, like how much time remained for the rest of them. If the baby had really died, they would just toss it in the corner with the other corpses. It was at the far end of the box, alongside the corner they used as a toilet. Together, the piles of death and filth filled the container with a stench that made it almost impossible to breathe and seemed to leech into the flesh. The terrible heat only made the smells worse. Yingjie had thrown his filthy clothes away two days before, but the smell had already become a part of him, just like the sweat and grime that had caked onto his skin. He feared he might never wash the smell away, but he also feared he might never have the chance to try.

The old man yelled something about his belly splitting, but Yingjie couldn't be bothered to listen. He pressed his ear to the wall and strained to hear what was happening outside. He could make out mechanical sounds, most likely dock machines. He wished he would hear somebody knock on the box's wall, checking to see if anybody was inside, but somewhere in his heart he knew that wouldn't happen.

The next time he dreamed of his mother, he fought against her as she tried to lead him to the box. She was too strong for him, though, and she shoved him inside as men dressed in black slammed the doors shut and locked them. He pounded against the metal walls until the skin of his hands split, but nobody would release him.

He woke again as people shoved against him, screaming not in hunger but in terror. He fought back at them. He had to before they crushed him in their panic. As he freed himself, he heard the old man again. The man was crying, his voice weak and pained.

Yingjie heard a strange ripping sound, and the elder fell silent. He realized the man hadn't been hungry at all.

The people around Yingjie froze, now quiet save a few pathetic whimpers. A wet, meaty sound—what might have been something small and terrible slipping free of its prison and hopping to the container's metal floor—filled his ears. A strange, high-pitched cry filled the box, followed by the expectant chattering of tiny teeth. The teeth sounded impossibly strong, and Yingjie could only imagine how sharp they might be.

The thing's cry reached a crescendo, and Yingjie heard the whispering rush of the creature leaping into the air. A woman erupted into fresh screams, and just underneath her cries of terror Yingjie could hear the shredding of flesh. The people around him burst into terrified motion. Somebody shoved Yingjie to the ground, and another stepped on him in an effort to escape. Through it all, the woman's dying screams peeled through the metal box. Yingjie heard the snapping of teeth and the soft, urgent sound of something feeding.

If Yingjie could dream of his mother one last time, he'd tell her he hated her.

Book Review

JUST LIKE HELL
Nate Southard
Thunderstorm Books

Nate Southard's debut is like a hard jab to the gut; his narrative voice can't be ignored. Writing with a visceral, sharp edge, he explores disturbing territory with an unflinching gaze. Readers will feel Dillon's bruises and cuts, slip in the blood, and then thank everything that's holy their lives aren't at the mercy of Southard's narrative whims.

Dillon Campbell had everything: a stellar future in football, waiting athletic scholarships, friends, and loyal teammates. He also had something else: a secret he dared share with no one, but which made him feel alive, complete, real—in a way all his athletic accolades never had. He thought he'd guarded this secret well… but he was wrong.

Someone knows, and now someone wants him to pay.

Dillon wakes in the dark, bound and gagged. Fear clogs his throat, and he realizes at once: he's been found out. He will pay a heavy price designed by someone without mercy or sympathy; a mind unhinged by rage. Before the end, Dillon will bathe himself in blood, and what he does may not be good or noble… but it will be justice.

A work like this is destined to be a future collector's item. Its truth is harsh and unpleasant, but necessary: the world is a dark place, and people do terrible things. The action is intense, pulse-pounding, and Southard's narrative style is lean, without feeling sparse. In classic novella fashion, he drops the reader into the midst of tumultuous plight, and then barrels towards the end, with few breathers along the way. Seeing Southard accomplish so much in such sort space makes the wait for his first full-length novel an eager one. — *Kevin Lucia*

MARIE O'REGAN
WORMWOOD: THE WORLD OF THE GREEN FAIRY

From the earliest references in ancient times to the modern, iconic images of Kylie Minogue as the Green Fairy in Baz Luhrmann's 2001 musical extravaganza Moulin Rouge, *absinthe's enduring image is irrevocably entwined with the artistic community and its worst excesses. It's thought of as a muse, a cure-all, an aphrodisiac and even as a bringer of creative vision. But what exactly is the truth?*

HOW ABSINTHE IS MADE

Absinthe as we know it today has only been in existence since the eighteenth century. Arguably its main ingredient, essence of wormwood, has been around far longer than that, though, as references can be found in the times of Ancient Rome and Greece. In those days, the most common way of taking it was to steep wormwood leaves in wine, and it was said to have many medicinal properties—Pliny the Elder was even known to have claimed it was an "elixir of youth." Hippocrates swore by it for menstrual cramps and as an aide in labour, he also claimed it cured jaundice and rheumatism. There are even references to it being used to cure tapeworm infections. As the years went by it was no longer limited to a medicine, and people drank it for pleasure. In mediaeval times it wasn't unusual to drink hot ale with wormwood added to it.

The absinthe we know today, though, is a different matter. It originated in Switzerland in the eighteenth century as a mix of several herbs: wormwood, anise and fennel, sometimes other herbs such as Melissa and hyssop steeped in alcohol—usually vodka. Ironically, the man who devel-

Albert Maignan's *Green Muse* (1895)

oped it, Dr. Pierre Ordinaire, did so in order to use it as a "remedy," but a more recreational use soon caught on.

The liquid formed from this first process is clear, and is known as absinthe bleu or blanche. To get its distinctive green colour, absinthe bleu has the herbs added to it once more, and the liquid is heated and distilled. As the herbs break down they release both their flavours and chlorophyll, the green pigment—and absinthe is made.

Absinthe made this way traditionally holds around a staggering seventy-two percent alcohol content, and for this reason it's usually diluted for drinking, unlike most spirits. Not to do so would be foolhardy, not to mention dangerous.

VIVE LA LOUCHE
HOW TO PREPARE ABSINTHE

There is a definite ritual associated with drinking absinthe. An absinthe glass (these are made with a "bubble" at the base to denote a measure) would be filled with a measure of absinthe. A measure was usually an ounce, but could sometimes be an ounce-and-a-half. A slotted spoon would sit across the top of the glass, with a sugar cube on it. Ice water would be poured very slowly over this, dissolving the sugar

> "ABSINTHE'S ENDURING IMAGE IS IRREVOCABLY ENTWINED WITH THE ARTISTIC COMMUNITY AND ITS WORST EXCESSES..."

into the absinthe solution. This process was known as "louching" the glass, and it allowed the absinthe's more subtle flavours (derived from the herbal oils) to be released, so that anise didn't dominate them. The proportion of absinthe to water should be approximately one part absinthe to four or five parts water.

Another way of preparing absinthe that became fashionable as its demand increased was the "absinthe fountain." Basically, this took the form of a big jug of iced water with spigots, or faucets, placed around its base. This allowed several customers to be served at once, and they would "louche" their own drink. The Olde Absinthe House in New Orleans' famed French Quarter was renowned for its marble fountains with brass faucets running along the length of the bar.

THE HISTORY OF THE GREEN FAIRY

The principle ingredient of absinthe is, as we've said, wormwood—and there is even a reference to wormwood in the Book of Revelation. "And the third angel sounded, and there fell a great star from heaven, burning as it were a lamp, and it fell upon the third part of the rivers, and upon the fountains of waters; And the name of the star is called Wormwood: and the third part of the waters became wormwood; and many men died of the waters, because they were made bitter." (Revelations 8:10 KJV). Obvi-

Grande wormwood, one of the three main herbs used in the production of absinthe.
Koehler's Medicinal-Plants (1887)

ously this far pre-dates absinthe, but there are those who have chosen to interpret the verse literally, especially as wormwood on its own is exceedingly bitter.

When Dr. Pierre Ordinaire first developed absinthe in Switzerland in the eighteenth century, it was for medicinal use as a remedy, or "tonic." Within a hundred years it had become enormously popular as an alcoholic drink, and achieved notoriety as a dangerously addictive, not to mention hallucinogenic, drink. Its nickname of the Green Fairy, or La Fée Verte, comes from this time—partly due to its colour, and partly due to its reputation as a "muse," inspiring creative genius in those who partook of it.

With the advent of mass production and the wine shortage in France of the 1880s it wasn't surprising that absinthe grew so quickly in popularity. It was even acceptable for women to drink in polite society. It was loved by all, and given publicity by the myriad of artists and writers in France at that time, it became synonymous with La Belle Époque, that golden period that spawned Impressionism and when Paris became home to writers and artists by the score. By the end of the nineteenth century, production in France alone had topped a million barrels a year.

It also made its way to the U.S., notably New Orleans, which was known then as little Paris—where it became fashionable under such names as Green Opal and Milky Way. Another name, Herbe Sainte, is still popular today.

Along with its increase in popularity, there was the inevitable backlash amongst the more conservative members of society, and the prohibitionists, caused by the excesses of some drinkers. In view of its predominance, it took the blame for public drunkenness, crime (there were two alcohol-related murders within a few months in 1905 and absinthe was blamed) and even violence and insanity. Small wonder then that in the early part of the twentieth century it was banned in several countries. Germany went so far as to ban distribution of the recipe. Aleister Crowley, when talking about those so intent on banning the Green Goddess, as he called it, said: "The Prohibitionist must always be a person of no moral character; for he cannot even conceive of the possibility of a man capable of resisting temptation. Still more, he is so obsessed, like the savage, by the fear of the unknown, that he regards alcohol as a fetish, necessarily alluring and tyrannical." Unfortunately, the prohibitionists won.

In the 1990s absinthe started to gain in popularity once more; this time outside France. Britain began to import it from countries that hadn't banned it, such as the Czech Republic, and the subsequent demand caused the French government to amend its original ban thus: only beverages labelled, literally, absinthe; or containing more thujone than the European Union guidelines permitted, were subject to the ban. This amendment allowed absinthe to be produced again, just so long as it was called a "wormwood-based

Edgar Degas' *L'Absinthe.*

liqueur" or "liqueur containing wormwood extract." Outside France, of course, it could, quite legitimately, be called absinthe. Manufacturers today, therefore, export its product as absinthe, whilst labelling the same product differently within France itself.

ABSINTHE:
ITS MYTHOLOGY AND EFFECTS

As has been mentioned already, the drinking of absinthe has been credited with many properties over the years; from curing ills (tapeworm, menstrual pains, rheumatism, jaundice, bad breath), to being an elixir of youth, to an aphrodisiac and even enhancing creative vision, opening the mind so that it can achieve its maximum creative potential. Its many artist and writer devotees have done nothing to demystify the drink.

Oscar Wilde once described the process of drinking absinthe. He said: "The first stage is like ordinary drinking, the second when you begin to see monstrous and cruel things. But if you can persevere you will enter in upon the third stage when you see things that you want to see." And that is where the secret of its appeal lies amongst the artistic community of that time. Wilde was a habitual drinker of absinthe, and once said it made his legs "feel like tulips"!

Wilde wasn't the only writer to be inspired by the Green Fairy. Ernest Hemingway loved the drink, calling it "brain-warming, idea-changing liquid alchemy," having been introduced to it whilst living in Spain. References to absinthe can be found in *For Whom The Bell Tolls* and *Death in the Afternoon*. This is also the name he gave to a cocktail he contributed to a 1930's recipe book, which consisted of absinthe drunk in the usual way—with the exception that, instead of water, champagne was used to dilute it. When asked about its effects,

Hemingway said: "The absinthe made everything seem better. I drank it without sugar in the dripping glass, and it was pleasantly bitter. I poured the water directly into it and stirred it instead of letting it drip. I stirred the ice around with a spoon in the brownish, cloudy mixture. I was very drunk. I was drunker than I ever remembered having been."

Another famous absinthe drinker was the French poet Arthur Rimbaud, who said, "When the poet's pain is soothed by a liquid jewel held in the sacred chalice, upon which rests the pierced spoon, the crystal sweetness, icy streams trickle down. The darkest forest melts into an open meadow. Waves of green seduce. Sanity surrendered, the soul spirals towards the murky depths, wherin lies the beautiful madness—absinthe." In later years Rimbaud seems to have turned away from absinthe, and indeed writing—living out his final years (at least until his premature death from cancer) engaged in gainful employment. His sometime partner, the poet Verlaine, was also a renowned drinker of absinthe, and much given to violent behaviour whilst under its influence. On one occasion he shot Rimbaud in the wrist, an act which not surprisingly ended the relationship.

Mary Shelley was reputed to be have been drinking absinthe along with her fiancé (and later husband), Percy Bysshe Shelley, their friend Lord Byron and his physician, John Polidori, and Mary's stepsister, Claire Clairmont, on holiday at the Villa Diodati by Lake Geneva in Switzerland when the inspiration for Frankenstein came. She wrote a short story that eventually became that novel—and that same

The Absinthe Drinker by Viktor Oliva (1861-1928)

night also served as inspiration to other members of her party. Byron wrote a partial story and discarded it, and it is this fragment that formed the basis of Polidori's most famous creation, "The Vampyre," which is widely regarded as the first modern vampire tale.

Many artists produced pieces devoted to the subject of absinthe. Manet's *The Absinthe Drinker*, Picasso's *Woman Drinking Absinthe* and his sculpture *Verre d'Absinthe*, Albert Maignan's *The Green Muse*, Degas' *L'Absinthe*… the list goes on, and there is even a short film, *Hasher's Delirium*, devoted to portraying the effects of absinthe, made in 1919 by early animator Emile Cole.

With the wealth of evidence, both anecdotal and in print from various sources, there is no doubt that absinthe is a powerful, highly popular drink. What makes it so different from other alcoholic tipples would seem to be that it produces a peculiarly clear-headed state of drunkenness, otherwise known as "lucid drunkenness." Referring back to Wilde's "third stage," it seems that although alcohol acts as a depressant, several of the herbs contained in absinthe act as stimulants—and it is this mix of ingredients that give rise to that famous stage, where the drinker would report simultaneously feeling very drunk, and very awake and aware. It is this "mind-opening" clarity felt by the drinker when in actual fact they are extremely drunk that has been the root of absinthe's reputation and mystique—and it is the devotion shown to it, and the creations accredited to its effects, that have perpetuated its aura of decadence. *Vive La Louche!*

An Interview with Brian Cartwright
by Norm Rubenstein

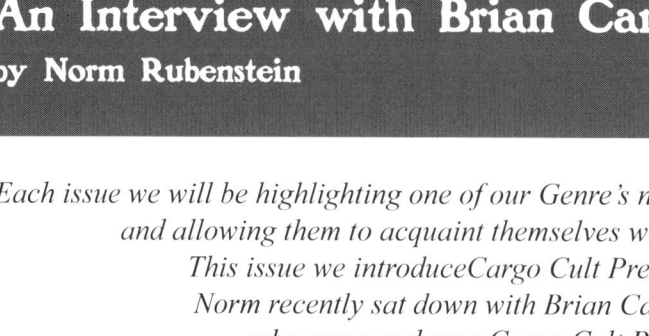

*Each issue we will be highlighting one of our Genre's newer Specialty Publishers and allowing them to acquaint themselves with our readers.
This issue we introduce Cargo Cult Press (CCP).
Norm recently sat down with Brian Cartwright,
who owns and runs Cargo Cult Press.*

NORM: Welcome, Brian. Why don't we begin with a bit about your background, and how Cargo Cult Press originated as a Specialty Press?

BRIAN: Brian Cartwright: My background? I'm a loudmouth Southerner who settled in the Arizona desert. I loved the novels of John Bellairs from a young age and as I got older my love for the strange, horrific and spooky pervaded my other interests. I remember *Castlevania* and *Eternal Darkness* were two favorite video games. Musically and aesthetically I resonated with the Goth crowd. There was something about lean cheekbones, clothes that were thirty years out of date, and those post-punk bass lines. I think a lot of the hardcore horror fans around my age would share my observations. I loved the Dell Abyss line, Poppy Brite, and *The Sandman*. This led into a more diverse exploration of darkness for me. I loved reading about the lives of the Beat writers almost as much as I enjoyed their writing. [David] Cronenberg led to [Alejandro] Jodorowsky and eventually the sublime Cremaster Cycle [by Matthew Barney]. I loved, and do love the horrific and surreal.

At the same time I developed a love for neat, well-ordered bodies of text. My first real job was laying out obituaries for my local newspaper at age sixteen. I remember during the 1996 Olympics I was scanning photos of the dead and condensing their lives to columns, while the sports guys were watching gymnasts hopping, three desks over. It was unreal. Later I worked for a hippy free weekly, worked for a role-playing game company, and did the early twenties bounce around. One of the things I did that I found the most satisfying was run a website called unwrite. That was a real joy. It featured short fiction, ongoing serials and some great blogs. What that really distilled for me was how much I enjoyed making stories look nice and picking great stories.

At the time, I hadn't really separated for myself the writing and editing. I got some solid advice from Weston Ochse, which helped me get a novella into strong enough shape to sell. But there was something missing. I hadn't been part of the other side of the creative process since unwrite, and I wanted that back. I did layout, marketing and wore a few hats at Bad Moon Books for Roy Robbins. It was fun and I got to meet a lot of people, but ultimately I was left empty by it. I didn't feel that I controlled a book's destiny. I wasn't giving interesting stories chances, or finding perfect art. I re-

Shroud Specialty Press Showcase: Cargo Cult Press

ally wanted more. I craved the chance to establish something special—carve out my spot. I sought out Larry Roberts and he provided invaluable advice. I observed how many new presses were starting up right now, and I didn't want to get lost in the mix. So with his guidance and my own intuition, I set out to do something different!

NORM: Is there any "story" behind, or particular reason that you chose the name Cargo Cult Press for your company?

BRIAN: The pretty version, or the "let's get real" version? Once I knew it was for real, I needed a name. Things were progressing with Wrath and I needed art for a book from David Niall Wilson. My wife and I racked our brains and came up with a ton of absolute dreck. Most weren't even worth mentioning. But one night sitting in my easy chair, drinking a mai tai, wearing an aloha shirt, I said "a-ha!"

I have a passion for the hyper-kinetic, technicolor, rum-soaked American perception of the South Pacific. It's always seemed so exotic, lurid, sexy and forbidden. Cannibals, one-hundred-year-old Japanese soldiers sitting in foxholes on Iwo Jima, mermaids, merchant marines, Elvis' *Blue Hawaii*, and of course, cargo cults. I remember seeing cargo cults in Mondo Cane and thinking, "WOW!" More than Las Vegas, Marrakech, Paris or Istanbul, I think the South Pacific represents the best of man's vivid imagination. Hopefully Cargo Cult Press is a name that evokes that.

NORM: CCP recently released its very first title, Wrath James White's Population Zero. Why did you decide upon this particular work as your inaugural release?

BRIAN: Because I wanted lots of hate mail and the occasional belligerent phone call? The small press has gotten lazy. When Shane Staley started Delirium Books, the small press was guilty of releasing a litany of overpriced reprints from the same eight-to-ten guys, and $45 copies of their slush piles. That doesn't cut it. Wrath James White is a brilliant writer who relentlessly pursues greatness. He is this century's Oscar Wilde. A master of simultaneously provoking thought and revolting, he is one of the most compelling writers working today. I asked him to push the envelope, and he did. No press is remembered for the chickenshit choices they made. *Population Zero* is relentless and beautiful, and I'll bet that by the time this article comes out, copies of the book are already selling for above cover price on eBay.

NORM: Is there anything concerning CCP's future plans and titles that you can share with the *Shroud Magazine* readers—what new titles do you have that you will be releasing over the next year that you can discuss?

BRIAN: I have some tremendous stuff coming out! There is *Remains* from Michael McBride very soon [see following review], and books from Brian Knight and Jeff Strand. Two of the writers I am most excited to be working with are Andersen Prunty and Gina Ranalli. Both are knockouts. Andy's *Sorrow King* may be the best book this year, and Gina's novel, *House of Fallen Trees*, is one of the best ghost stories I have read. By the time this article appears, I should have launched a lettered-only series, and have another digital chapbook out. For later in the year I have a novel from two small-press heavies writing together, and I always leave a slot opening in case a "must sign" book shows up.

NORM: You just mentioned a second digital chapbook. Could you perhaps tell our readers just what these represent and contain, and why you decided to produce them in the first place? Also, I believe that Gina Ranalli's *Skin Flowers* was Cargo Cult Press' first such digital chapbook? Have you been happy with this title? Oh, and of course, I wouldn't be the infamous, yet intrepid, super-nag of an interviewer if I didn't ask you to spill the beans and give us some further information as to at least who the author of this second digital chapbook is going to be, if not the actual title as well?

BRIAN: Glad you asked! The digital chapbook is the obvious extension of the current print chappie. With the increase in fuel and printing costs, paperbound chapbooks become increasingly cost prohibitive. With digital implementation you can pass the savings directly on to the reader. What would be a $15 dollar paperbound book becomes a $3-4 digital piece. Right now what excites me the most about digital and this genre is it drawing new customers. We're seeing new people buying these. And for your information, Mr. Super-Nag, our second such digital chapbook will be from Andersen Prunty. It's entitled *The Night The Moon Made a Sound*.

NORM: One of the things that endeared so many collectors to recent presses has been low limitation releases like Delirium's *Ultras* or Earthling's *Mr. Dark's Carnival*. Will CCP have any such super low limitations coming out?

BRIAN: Nothing too drastic. I will be launching a line of lettered-only releases. The first one is a novella from Andy Prunty entitled *Market Adjustment* that will be slipcased. I also have a lettered edition of a hot novel being released later this year that the original publisher will not be doing as a lettered.

NORM: What differentiates your Lettered editions from your Limited editions, and what considerations go into their respective designs and construction?

BRIAN: The guiding principle of both is to be better than the other guys. The average is a $50 book that looks like a $25 dollar book. So many lettereds are the same ugly book in a fucking traycase. That is lipstick on a pig. I kneel at the feet of my masters, and those that inspire me: Bloodletting Press, Charnel House and Arion Press. Beautiful, worthy volumes that enhance a library regardless of the focus of the collection. If I am selling a book for $50, I want it to look like a $100 book. I am really proud of *Population Zero*. It's striking. Pulled off a shelf, it is instantly recognizable. As to my lettereds? Asking a customer to spend $150-1,000 on a book is asking them to show faith. I want to reward that faith. Fine materials, good construction. I think I am hitting my goals if people buy my horror books and become general bibliophiles.

NORM: Thanks for the fascinating Interview, Brian. Anything else, in closing, that you'd like to say or share with *Shroud* readers?

BRIAN: Yes—Thanks for reading *Shroud*! 2009 is going to rock, but 2010 will blow it out of the water. Let me leave you with one word to watch for in the future; Hubris. It's going to be huge.

After speaking with Brian Cartwright for a length of time, one becomes convinced of his sincerity. Here is a man who is driven; a knowledgeable perfectionist, who combines a solid vision and business plan, who loves both books and the horror genre, and who wants to combine the very best aspects of his two loves (in addition to his love for his beautiful and supportive wife, Beth) into Cargo Cult Press. He is charming, funny and approachable, and very supportive of the many fans and readers of horror who he hopes will embrace his publishing efforts.

As this article is being written, CCP is about to release its first general sales title, Wrath James White's *Population Zero*. I've been allowed to read both Population Zero and CCP's subsequent announced release, *Remains*, by Michael McBride, which should be released around the same time as this issue of *Shroud Magazine*, and to share some of the artwork from both novels with you. An examination and review of these two initial title choices of Brian Cartwright's for release by Cargo Cult Press should provide some additional insight as to the man and the Press, and how excited horror genre readers should be over this new specialty press and its books.

It is hard to fault Cartwright's selection of Wrath James White as Cargo Cult Press' inaugural author. Over the past seven years, this Las Vegas based author, former professional fighter and current fight trainer has risen to the very forefront of the horror genre by presenting a unique literary style that is as hard-hitting as any of the knockout punches he used to deliver. Wrath combines an intelligent, witty and very provocative examination of philosophical, societal, religious and political issues along with extreme sensuality, violence and eviscerating, primal horror. All of this is properly showcased within the pages of *Population Zero*, which is Wrath James White writing at the peak of his form. While perhaps not appropriate for elementary school age children, or those weak of heart or stomach, this book is almost required reading for the well read and adventurous horror fan.

Tom Moran Cover Art for *Population Zero*.

Population Zero introduces us to the story's protagonist, Todd Hammerstein. Todd is a nice, skinny, red-haired young man. Seemingly ordinary, Todd is concerned about our planet and the environment. Todd's two favorite magazines are Vegan Times and Imperiled Planet. He eats neither meat nor dairy, runs every day, and not only does not own an automobile by choice, he rides his bicycle six miles each way to work. Todd works for the State Welfare Department. He spends his days reviewing and processing claims for monetary support from a never-ending line of people seeking financial assistance and/or medical assistance and/or food stamps from the government. This daily grind is beginning to have an effect upon Todd.

Todd has recently become an adherent and devout member of a new extreme environmental action organization, some would say cult, called Zero Population. Based upon the best-selling book of the same name written by the group's founder, Heimlich Anattoli, the group advocates saving the Earth through the voluntary sterilization of all humans. Indeed, Anattoli has previously authored another best selling book, titled *The Human Plague*. Todd is true to his mentor, proudly having not only recently had a vasectomy, but also convincing one of his co-workers to have the same procedure performed. Todd's problems commence when he decides that all that he had done, and is currently achieving, to reduce population growth is just not enough. A desperate and despondent Todd decides to try a new method of decreasing the supply of future children by using a combination of bribery and intimidation to coerce potential aid recipients to agree to, depending upon their sex, either have their tubes tied or have a vasectomy (and if a pregnant female, to also undergo an immediate abortion) in exchange for future and permanent no-hassle government financial assistance. Todd's initial efforts are careful and even timorous, but as he begins to encounter success and observe the very real power he has over those seeking governmental financial assistance, he grows bolder and more confident.

Of course, this being a story by Wrath James White, there's even more to this than already meets the eye. Todd, himself, is a wildcard. On one fateful day, when Todd was twelve years old, he made an innocent yet fateful comment to his mother. Noting her increased weight and the now obvious bulge in her belly that had apparently been previously hidden by her carefully chosen attire, Todd asked his mom if she might be pregnant. This precipitates a truly horrific train of events, chillingly and graphically detailed by author White, that ultimately result in a shocking lifetime trauma to the poor child. This, in turn, acts to help explain what transpires once Todd's plans to help his mentor and Zero Population achieve their goals goes awfully awry. The body count begins to rise and Todd suddenly finds himself running for his very life.

The book's pacing is fierce, and even the secondary characters like Todd's ex-girlfriend, Stephanie, and her new roommate, the Amazonian, female bounty-hunter and would-be Terminator (or is it Terminatrix), Cathy, among many others, are brought deftly to life with wry humor by the author. In *Population Zero*, White deals with many contemporary issues that are very much newsworthy now, and doesn't tread lightly while doing so. The book is certainly, and justifiably, controversial. However, though White is explicit in his prose, he is agile and subversively thoughtful and thought provoking in his examination of these highly charged issues. The story remains a true page-turner from its first paragraph straight through to its very last sentence. *Population Zero* is an exceptional adult horror story for the 21st century, and one hell of a great beginning for new horror publisher Cargo Cult Press. Kudos and congratulations to both Brian Cartwright, and especially to Wrath James White, for such an impressive book.

How does one follow-up such an auspicious debut as Cargo Cult Press has achieved with its inaugural title, *Population Zero*? Well, Brian Cartwright has decided to do so by turning to brilliant veteran horror author Michael McBride, who has written a short novel, *Remains*, which should be released by CCP in February 2009. The story's premise is fascinating: On May 21, 2007, seven religious studies graduate students from the University of Colorado at Boulder rent three cabins in the Colorado wilderness on the Western edge of the continental divide, twenty-seven miles from the closest town of Pine Springs. They are on a journey in search of God. They believe that they have discovered actual clues, within the Bible, that pinpoint the true location of the Nephilim, the "dark angels" who, with Satan, were cast down out of Heaven by God and imprisoned within the Earth.

Artwork by Tom Moran for *Remains*.

They hope that by actually locating and finding these Nephilim, they, at least by inference and association, also prove the existence of God. They are all computer savvy, and have set up a daily computer blog, where they can remain in contact with their various family and loved ones. All seems well as of July 11, 2007, when their last blog is posted. However, all contact is suddenly lost after that, and when a Forest Ranger checks in on the cabins on July 14th, he finds that while all supplies, food and clothing remain, the seven students have disappeared without any trace. Subsequent mass searches of the surrounding forest and countryside find absolutely nothing, and on the first anniversary of their disappearance, July 11, 2008, a ten foot high cross is quietly raised on the summit of nearby Mount Isolation with a bronze plaque listing the names of the seven missing students along with the short phrase, "Seek and ye shall find."

However, on October 29, 2009, a landowner in the area who raises Alpacas illegally hunts down and kills a large mountain lion who had already attacked and eaten three of his $20,000 per head Alpacas—only to find that the mountain lion had also recently been feasting upon a human femur. After DNA testing reveals the femur belongs to one of the seven missing students, Brent Cavenaugh, a police detective with the Denver Police Department, and older brother of another of the seven missing students, contacts the remaining relatives of the missing students and puts together and equips an expedition to the very same cabins that the missing students had been living in at the time of their disappearance. Joining Detective Cavenaugh are the father of one missing student, the two elder sisters of two more of the missing students and the two elder brothers of the remaining two students. The six grieving relatives try and work together to discover the ultimate fate of the missing students, as a nasty early winter storm settles down over the remote area, effectively shutting the six off from the rest of the world, and stranding them at the cabin site. Oh, and one more thing—the student's femur and the dead mountain lion's carcass both tested positive for a very exotic, extremophile micro. The only known form of this specific species on Earth is the dead fossilized samples found in the famous Martian meteorite examined by Earth's scientists. Yet, the specimens found on both the femur and inside the mountain lion are very much alive.

Artwork by Tom Moran for *Remains*.

Remains is, like *Population Zero*, another expertly written page-turner that you will find difficult to put down. Author McBride quickly sets up his premise, introduces his cast of characters, and then takes the readers on a thrilling amusement park ride that maintains a barely sub-light cruising speed as the readers are presented with enough clever plot twists and red herrings to do Agatha Christie proud. Indeed, as the gruesome death count begins to mount and the members of the expedition meet their various untimely and unpleasant ends, the story will remind some of Christie's justly famous and classic *Ten Little Indians aka And Then There Were None*. In *Remains*, the writing and story have been modernized and are far more explicit, but the writing contains a similar underlying innate satiric wit and intelligence. The book is a truly entertaining read that will keep you guessing until literally the final page, and the ultimate revelation is worthy of all its buildup, and almost begs for a further examination in what would be a most enjoyable sequel. The book is further well served and enhanced by the brilliant artwork of the very talented artist Tom Moran, who also did all the striking artwork for *Population Zero*, and that is superbly reproduced by CCP throughout the books.

Cargo Cult Press displays a level of commitment to its readers and a degree of craftsmanship in the books it is releasing that bodes very well both for the specialty press and for readers of the horror genre. Brian Cartwright has certainly raised the bar for the entire genre's press, and Cargo Cult Press is therefore certainly deserving of such support. Look for great things from this Publisher over the next year and onwards.

Ghostly Footsteps

Norman A. Rubin

Memories of the past are usually quite pleasant but one bit of memory that was and is still constantly retained in my mind sent a cold finger of terror down my spine that left me agitated. About a year ago I was staying overnight at the old Bristol Hotel, an aged rather obsolete lodging. There a strange incident occurred that was beyond my wildest expectations. A ghostly figure was my companion that night that put me in a state of fear. I imagined that it came through a frightening nightmare, but was it only a terrible dream or an actual happening.

A business engagement called and I was obliged to make a stopover in that city. The choice of hotels was limited as the city played host to athletic games, and hotel rooms were filled to capacity with the participants and fans to the games. Thus, I was obliged to register for a room at that hostel, an ancient edifice of four stories, weather-darkened and solitary, brick and stone squeezed on every side by the overgrowing of the great city, with endowments of the past years.

But the mysteries that happened that night still haunt me. Listen to my story and you will understand….

When I registered at reception desk I was given the key to a room on the second floor, which seemed to be the only vacant one in the entire hotel. Yet, when walked to the dimly lit corridor to the creaky elevator I saw no one about, not a soul greeted me. When I alighted from the lift on the second floor and made my way to my room through the dimly lit corridor, I heard no sound to suggest occupancy of the rooms. It was strange as it was early in the evening when people prepared for their nightly entertainment or whatever engagement awaited their interest.

The room that I entered for my evening's lodging was as ancient in furnishing as the hotel itself. When I switched on the dim overhead light I noticed a bed of solid oak, a heavy armchair from another era, night table with a lamp, and a wardrobe heavy and cumbersome. One thing that was disturbing was a large painting facing the bed that was of rather strange dimensions, picturing a scene with a flowery garden with nymphs dancing to the pan pipes of the satyrs; other strange mythical creatures were all around in the canvas. The disturbing part of the painting was a black attired figure centered in that garden, grim in facial features and his black hair long and stringy like strands of willow sprigs; he looked like a haunted man that endured ridicule and chafing during his life. He seemed to be the devil incarnate that orchestrated all that occurred in the garden.

I dismissed all that I had seen and imagined, as I was quite tired from my journey and a bit bilious from a frugal supper at a nondescript restaurant. The weather was rather blustery with the wind

> "The disturbing part of the painting was a black attired figure centered in that garden…"

blowing shrill and shrewd, and the night air damp with expected rain with the going down of the blurred sun. The only thought in mind was an early night's rest. Preparations were in order; a warm shower was welcomed even though the water sluggishly gurgled through the pipes; then into my clean pajamas and the warm embrace of the bed.

The bed fortunately was quite comfortable with a firm mattress, clean sheets and warm blankets. I had taken a book to read, but the comfort and warmth of the bed soon lulled me into a sound sleep. Yet through the dark of night at the toll of midnight I was rudely awakened by the loud sound of footsteps with clear tap of high-heeled shoes walking slowly past my door, then after walking to the end of the corridor, they began to return and repeat the route twice over.

I commented to myself that it was a damn nuisance and quite rude of that impolite person who had no regard for the other guests. Yet firm action on my part should be attended. I switched on the table lamp, cursed when I noted the late hour on my watch, and, lifting myself from the bed, I made for the door to the room. A touch of anger was on my lips when I opened the door, but to my surprise the sound of the footsteps had faded away, and when I looked about the dim corridor I was greeted with emptiness.

After a moment or two of searching with my eyes, I pulled back to my room and relocked the door. But, when I was returning to the comfort of my bed and by chance I had a look at the painting, I saw the grim faced figured had disappeared from the center. I was quite puzzled and looked deeper into the painting, but the figure was nowhere to be seen on the canvas. I contemplated the strangeness of the disappearance of the figure, but shrugged it off to be a figment of my imagination.

I returned to my bed and the continuance of my sleep, but upon the close of my eyes a nightmare enveloped me into a disturbing scene. It pictured my body with satyr cloven hooves and a horned head playing the pan and dancing with lovely nymphs. Yet the features on my face were not of joy but of grim countenance.

Suddenly, within my horrible nightmare, I was aware of loud footsteps coming along the corridor outside, followed by the sound of a chain being dragged along. I was depicted as being very frightened as I was seemingly alone on the second floor. The terrifying dream pictured me lying in dread, hoping the footsteps would go away, but to my horror I saw the door slowly pushed open, and whatever it was entered dragging a chain. Slowly it walked into the room, and I noticed it was that grim faced figure that disappeared from the painting. It was the same black attired figure, an indefinably grim person that was hounded by images that stole from their retreats, in the likeness of forms and faces from the past and from the grave.

How long this spirit remained in my room, but when he moved about the room he was searching for something unknown. The he turned and looked with a haunted gaze; his voice, low speaking, deep and grave, seemed to set to questioning me. It was the voice of a haunted man in search of the dark deep gulf of the past, slowly receding in the dark of the nightly hour. Relief was etched on my face when I heard the movement of the sound of ghostly footsteps, followed by the clinking of the dragging chain, retracing its passage to the door of the room. Then it slowly it simply walked through the wood to the corridor and the sounds slowly faded away.

I awoke with a start in a cold sweat from the nightmare when daylight streamed into the room through the slight opening of the heavy curtains. I didn't know if this nightmare could have any meaning, or whether it was real or not, but I knew that the figure was not a ghost of any description, but the footsteps were human, so I thought, and the chinking of the chain was still audible.

Yet, when I allowed more daylight to enter the room, I chanced to look at the painting. To my surprise, the black attired figure was there in the center of the canvas, grim as ever. Then I saw, to my horror, faint footprints on the on the floor leading from the door and returning; It etched a note of fear as they were of cloven hooves.

However, I was quite sure of what occurred during the night, frightening in all its proportions, so did not prolong my stay at the Bristol Hotel. There was no banter of enquiry at the reception desk when I returned the key to the room. But, when I was handed the receipt for payment, I was quite shocked when I noticed the receptionist to be a black attired figure with features indefinably grim....

Norman A. Rubin is a retired former correspondent for the Continental News Service (USA), and keeps himself busy writing short stories and articles of all genres.

Excerpt from Hiram Grange & the Nymphs of Krakow
Hiram Grange & the Beast of the Air
Richard Wright

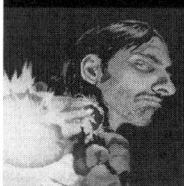

Hiram slammed through the door into the cinema bar, whipping it shut on the corridor behind him. Something heavy hit hard from the other side, staggering him forward, and he threw his weight back, sneering through the fear as he forced it slowly flush. Door closed, his legs straining as he tried to stop his feet slipping beneath the vast strength trying to knock him aside, he scanned the room. No staff, no customers, just bottles and bottles of sweet beers and spirits, calling him over.

"Later, my dears," he told them through gritted teeth. "I'm a tad busy."

It should have been such a simple kill. A name, a place, a little background - more than he was often given when Mrs Bothwell issued his assignments. His current predicament was of his own design, bred of complacency and distraction. The Man in the Bad Hat had even tried warning him, but to no avail. Hiram had struggled to focus on the task in hand, and it was all the fault of that bitch, Kedra. After dogging his tracks for months, a lean shadow who had hauled his wiry arse out of more than one fire unasked, she had finally chosen to step into the light. At first she had entranced him. Her square shoulders and lean body, small firm breasts perfect beneath leather, were a scarred reminder of his one true love, Jodie. While the actress had yet to recognise her feelings for him, he had dallied with the notion that this woman, Gabrysia, could satisfy him in her absence.

And within minutes of conversation she had torn his world apart with elaborate fantasies of secret organisations and hierarchies. Lies and fabrications, clearly wrought to unnerve and unbalance him, but to what end?

It pushed again, and he cried out, his strength fading fast. Even now, she distracted him, and he needed to focus, to devise a solution. It was massive, many times stronger than he was. Simple physics told him he was going to lose this inverted tug of war. Sweat dripped down his roman nose. There was one exit from the bar, and he was wrestling to keep that shut. He couldn't see a fire door. He would remember to discuss that with the health and safety people, should he meet them in the afterlife. The windows looked like reinforced glass, and he was four storeys up.

A flimsy panel of wood away, the thing screeched in frustration. The sound, impossibly shrill, pierced him like a sharp and tearing blade. He collapsed to the floor, doubling up as something delicate ruptured inside him. Bottles shattered along the bar like they were being raked with automatic fire, casting glass and fluids of all colours and tastes across the room. The windows blew outwards with an elegance worthy of slow motion. Scarlet warmth burst from his ears and nose.

A werebat. Of all the fucking things to expect. When Hiram first saw it in front of the cinema screen, first heard it tear the air in two, he had silently congratulated the movie's special effects team, even as he dropped his Webley, tooled up with silver bullets, in order to clutch his ears. He had last seen the gun sliding beneath a bank of seats, as he cursed Bothwell for her lack of specificity. *Lycanthrope*, she told him. Of course he'd assumed it would be a wolf.

A final push.

He was still on the floor, prone, unable to stop the door from opening.

It stepped into the bar, the stench of wet fur and death rolling ahead of it.

The windows were blown out.

He was on the fourth floor.

A muscular flex of wings, an impression of hair and teeth above him.

Pushing himself to his feet, Hiram bolted. Claws raked the back of his suit jacket as he went, slicing skin and drawing a scream from him. His foot hit the window edge, glass shards penetrating his sole.

Four storeys up, Hiram erupted into the night sky, the sense of space, of void, crushing his sense of self, and he prayed to whatever gods might still consider his worth.

And a dark and shrieking winged thing followed close behind him.

Mrs Bothwell waited politely for the still screaming cinema audience to trample one another onto the street, wondering how much they had seen in the gloom of the auditorium. Hiram had been fast, arresting the beast's attention before it could decide on a victim, and drawing it away. She doubted that any two witnesses would give the same story to the authorities, if any of them could manage a coherent account at all, and that suited her to perfection. Reliable witnesses would need to be attended to carefully, for fear of setting panic free in the streets. Her people called it containment. The world was not ready to know of the shadow things that flitted in and out of it, or the struggles that waged on the edge of a reality far more fragile than most of mankind could accept.

She patted her trim, practical handbag, feeling Hiram's precious Webley nestled amongst her tissues. She had watched him lose the weapon with pursed lips. The opportunity to see him in action was a rare thing - it was her job to point him towards danger, not trot along after like some eager cheerleader - and she had to confess that deep down she was

Malcolm McClinton

disappointed. How he intended to dispatch this foe without the barrel full of silver bullets he had managed to acquire was beyond her. No doubt he would find a way. Improvisation was one of his great gifts, and had made him the longest lived agent she had recruited. Caleb had been the shortest, she remembered. Two weeks. Barely time to learn how to point and shoot. Her superiors had not been impressed, and for a while she had believed that they might be considering her expendability. Then she found Hiram, and her status improved. No wonder she was fond of him.

An elbow caught her between the ribs, a straggler putting his own safety before that of this thin, prim old lady before him. No manners at all. She flicked her wrist, rotating the umbrella in her hand one hundred and eighty degrees, where the weighted tip crashed into his temple with force enough to drop him like a sack of potatoes. The man, a bruiser at six foot, with a boxer's build, hit the floor at her feet and lay there twitching, a low groan drooling from his lips. Lesson learned. Courtesy cost nothing.

Behind her, three confused members of staff watched her warily, too confused by the stampede to challenge her. She gave a matronly smile and left them to their anxious bemusement. However Hiram intended to finish the job, he would not risk bringing the creature back through the multiplex, so it was safe enough to leave them where they were and wait for him in the street.

As she stepped onto the sidewalk, crowded with those previously desperate escapees now deciding to fulfil the role of idiot crowd, she heard glass shatter above her head. The mentally deficient around her looked up, as though the situation really merited full assessment. Mrs Bothwell popped open her umbrella and raised it above her head. A second later the thud and patter of broken glass vibrated through her canopy, and the rest of the crowd were showered with tiny, slicing shards of pain.

More screaming and aimless running, away from her this time, and she saw blood dripping from fresh wounds. It all looked superficial enough, and with luck would be sufficient to hasten them out of the general area. With the last of the glass pattering at her feet, she closed the brolly and looked up. Hiram was dropping towards her like a stone, arms outstretched as though they could slow his descent. The bat plummeted after, wings drawn in as it bared the dozens of teeth in it's wrinkled, mortar shell maw.

She raised her eyebrows and stepped back, certain they would crash right into her. As the werebat caught up to him, barely ten feet above her, it extended its wings with a crack, arresting its descent as it snapped at its prey.

Hiram caught her eye, and there was a second of recognition and surprise on his narrow face.

Then he twisted, throwing his arms around the werebat's neck and flipping his legs around its waist. The creature shrieked, bore down with those great wings, and drove them back into the sky.

Mrs Bothwell stared as the wind from the downthrust flattened her hair. If she had reached out, she could almost have touched them. She watched them gain erratic height, the bat frantically trying to scratch away its new passenger. With a sigh, she pulled her phone from her bag. It seemed there were going to be some containment issues after all.

As the city span around him, a bewildering kaleidoscope of lights, Hiram hung on to the creature's neck for dear life, pulling himself cheek to cheek to avoid its massive, drooling maw. One bite was all it would take to consign him to a winged doom amidst the spires and towers of the city. In the seconds since he had seized the creature he had lost his sense of direction, and knew only that they were rising fast. It shrieked, and the noise jabbed down his spine. His legs jerked in response, but he held tight, feeling the muscles beneath the foul smelling fur roil as it struggled to keep them both aloft. Sudden winds slapped him, and while he couldn't risk a glance, he guessed that they had cleared the height of the building.

Claws raked his side, ripping up flesh along his ribs, and he gave a shriek of his own, pitiful and human next to the bat's brain-freezing cries. This couldn't go on forever. Soon enough, the bat would realise that it only had to put down on the nearest brown-stone, and it could tear him apart at its leisure. He needed a plan.

He didn't have one, and so settled on changing the dynamic a little, hoping that new opportunities would present themselves.

Hugging the bat to him with his left arm, he flicked his right out to one side. As the knife shot forth from the forearm sheath he had been wearing since New Orleans, he had a moment of panic, believing absolutely that he had misjudged the timing, and his last remaining weapon was plummeting to the street below. When his fingers closed around the handle, he relaxed more than should have been possible, so far above the hard streets. Loosening his grip, he drew back, feeling the bat tense in anticipation of a clear bite at his face. For the briefest second, they were eye to eye. It was grinning.

Hiram grinned back, and slid his knife into its right eye. It spasmed, wrenching back with unwitting force, and his legs lost purchase on the creature's waist. He swung towards the street, heart pounding for a weightless moment as he caught himself on a wet fistful of fur at its neck, letting his own momentum swing him around until he could grasp the handle of his own blade with his other hand. The bat snapped feebly at his face. It missed, and rank drool splattered his face, the smell of rotten meat diving into his nostrils as they thrashed in the air. Tumbling now, he caught a glimpse of the street as they rolled around each other, horribly close, traffic stopped as faces peered up at him. He wondered if they could see his stomach, which he could only imagine was somewhere far above, following them towards a two-dimensional end.

He calculated his chances of survival. It wasn't complex math.

The bat's wings stiffened, and their plummet slowed so abruptly that he almost lost his grip again. The drop snapped into a fast, shallow glide along the street, still bound for the ground. They shot along above the traffic, the bat still dazed as they dipped down, weaving between the vehicles, and then Hiram's dangling heels smacked the road, bouncing up, then smacking down one more time, hard enough to drag him from his nemesis, crashing him to the tarmac. Momentum skidded him further, and he rolled to gain some control. A rib snapped, popping dully inside him, blooming fire through his insides.

At last he stopped, sprawled on the road, barely able to comprehend that moments ago he had been far above. He longed for the luxurious embrace of unconsciousness. An ambulance would complete the picture perfectly. There would be drugs in an ambulance. An ambulance crew too, but there lay the problem. Where ambulance crews appeared, police officers often followed, and he couldn't be around when they did so. Sitting up, hissing as his broken rib stabbed him, he shook his head to clear his doubled vision. There were people gathering, their faces gaining definition as his eyes focused. Some were concerned, but others were curious, and these worried him. Curious people intervened.

"You okay, buddy?" The question came from an overweight Caucasian in a rumpled suit. There was lipstick on his collar, and Hiram wondered if it had been put there by a wife, or a mistress.

"Where did it go?"

"Where did what go?"

Hiram took a steadying breath and stood, his left leg barely able to take weight at all. "Surely you aren't mocking me, sir?" Regardless how torn and bloodied he felt, or perhaps because that was the precise picture he presented, the man stepped back, his face a little whiter than before, and he nodded along the street. Hiram saw the bat, thirty metres on. It had slammed into the side of a vacated yellow taxi, crumpling the door, and lay prone on the ground, neck twisted at so sharp an angle that a sympathetic shudder went down his back. The involuntary movement was enough to buckle his weak leg, and he went down on one knee, teeth clenched as little explosions of pain popped his hip. The recovery time from this little skirmish was something he looked forward to very much. His pipe would be close to hand, as would Mistress Absinthe. And girls. He would find girls, and make them wear uniforms.

"Buddy?"

Hiram ignored the distant voice as the world greyed along the edges of his vision. Girls. Uniforms. Absolutely.

"Buddy, it's still kicking. You hear me? I just saw it move."

"You kill it then." Why were the sheep always so willing to step back and let him save them? The bat was crippled, barely conscious, and still they waited for him to dispatch it. He took a deep breath, coughing it back out and tasting blood in his throat. The bat lay as he last saw it, but as he watched, it jerked its head, trying to realign its spine. The movement was feeble, but would soon grow in strength. Only one thing could put a lycanthrope down with any permanence. Trapping his own whimper in his throat, aware of his growing audience, he pushed to his feet, rocking on his heels for a second before stumbling forwards. Momentum and gravity kept him moving, despite the objections of the flesh.

The bat growled deep in its throat as he reached it, a quiver running along one outstretched wing as it scented his presence. Hiram flicked his wrist, then stared at his empty fingers, wondering where his knife was. "Ah yes," he said, feeling giddy and strange. "My apologies." Leaning down, he grabbed the handle of his knife, still embedded in the bat's eye socket. Giving a brutal twist of the blade to reopen the already healing wound, he jerked it free. The bat arched its back, wings flexing feebly as Hiram pulled his keys from his pocket. Struggling to focus, he pinched off the silver *I Love Dublin* fob that he had picked up in Ireland. The bat sensed the proximity of the metal, and tensed for a final bid for freedom.

Hiram dropped the fob into the bat's moist, gaping eye socket, and it stilled as the silver did its instant work.

Hiram smiled, then frowned when he couldn't straighten up again. He heard far off sirens wailing, but his body's insistence that everything stop immediately rolled over him, and he collapsed across his prey, dead to the world.

"He looks so weak, lying there."

"Your opinion was not invited."

"Are you certain he can do this?"

"Are you volunteering to take his place?"

"Of course not."

"Then cease your gabble and get him in the car. The police are almost here."

"As you wish."

"Gently. You're going to fix him up. That doesn't mean you can break him first."

"He needs more than field treatment."

"It's all he's getting. Make it count."

To be continued in
Hiram Grange & the Nymphs of Krakow....

Richard Wright is a scribbler of horror and other dark fictions, and his novels, stories and plays have been published and performed on both sides of the Atlantic. He has lived in Scotland for over a decade, and for most of that time has been writing one thing or another.

Richard's writings have recently appeared in the anthologies *Doctor Who: Short Trips - Transmissions*, *Beneath the Surface*, *Tattered Souls* and *Choices*, among others. His plays, *Black Hearts* and *Haunter*, toured Scotland.

Discover more on Richard on the web at *www.richardwright.org*.

Shroud Submission Guidelines

Fiction: Shroud considers horror, dark mystery, dark fantasy and suspense short stories up to 5,000 words. In addition, we are interested in tightly woven flash fiction, and (in some cases) serialized novellas. Thriller and Suspense tales with a horror aspect are also welcome. We HIGHLY recommend that you buy a SAMPLE ISSUE in order to get a clear idea of our style and tone.

We are especially interested in:

Mythic horror in a real world setting; Classically-themed horror and suspense; Supernatural horror; Creature horror; Dark Fantasy in a contemporary/RW setting; Noir with a horror element.

We are LESS interested in:

Hard Science Fiction; Sword and Sorcery or anything set in a fantasy world; Stories about serial killers; Vampires ala Rice; First person accounts.

Submission Format: Send us electronic submissions in .DOC or .RTF format as a file attachment. Your subject line should clearly say "SUBMISSION". Simultaneous submissions are NOT okay. Please do not send us multiple submissions -- please only send us one story at a time and do not send your next submission until we give you a reply to the first. Reprints are fine provided they have not been published within three months and the author currently bears the copyright. A short bio would be nice, including any awards or published credits, however your story will stand on its own merit.

Response Time: For our open submission reading periods, please refer to our website at *www.shroudmagazine.com*. Response time averages 2 to 4 months, but stories kept for further consideration by the editors may take additional time.

IMPORTANT: If you have NOT received an acknowledgment of receipt for your SHORT STORY within 1-5 Days of your submission then it is likely the submission was formatted incorrectly. We do appreciate your hard efforts and your creative vision, but with more than 350 submissions a month, if your submission is incorrectly formatted then it will be (unfortunately) deleted... sorry.

Artwork: Please query with samples. We are actively looking for talented artists for covers and B&W interior illustrations.

Nonfiction: Looking for well-researched stories on supernatural phenomenon, dark music, art, and interviews of key players within the genre, film reviews, game reviews. Query first.

Payment: Shroud will pay a flat rate of $10 for Flash Fiction, $25 for fiction up to 5000 words, and $25 for nonfiction up to 3000 words. Book reviews and other pieces will be discussed with the authors on a case-by-case basis.

Submission Guidelines (continued)

Anthologies: We automatically consider all fiction submissions for our active anthologies. If accepted, Shroud pays .01 cents a word plus two copies of the published collection.

Send to: editor@shroudmagazine.com

Novels and Novellas

Shroud publishing is interested in building a catalog of intelligent dark fiction novels and novellas. If you have a COMPLETED manuscript or a series of short fiction, please query with a short synopsis and one sample chapter. Send to the editor.

A note on novel and novella submissions: We are a small press. We have a small press budget. If we are able to put your novel or novella into print we will do our best to market and distribute it, but the likelihood of you or us getting rich is very slim. Consider long and hard before you submit to us. We do not offer advances and our royalty rates will be modest. Having said that, if accepted, we will edit, design, layout your book, get it printed, sell it direct, and do our very best to get it distributed through a major distributor. WE will incur all of the aforementioned expenses, not you. We will never charge you for reading or publishing your book. Nor should you ever be charged.

So, if this works for you, we'd love to see your novel/novella.

Response time for novels/novellas could be 3-6 months as our reading time permits.

For more information about Shroud please visit our website at:

WWW.SHROUDMAGAZINE.COM

See our publications, join our forums, send suggestions, and more.

Made in the USA